Rose Zwi was born in Mexico, lived in London and Israel, but spent most of her life in South Africa. She has lived in Australia since 1988. She has won several prizes for her work, including *Another Year in Africa*, *Last Walk in Naryshkin Park* and *Safe Houses*.

Speak the Truth, Laughing

Nine stories and a novella, *House Arrest*

Rose Zwi

SPINIFEX

Spinifex Press Pty Ltd
504 Queensberry Street
North Melbourne, Vic. 3051
Australia
women@spinifexpresss.com.au
http://www.spinifexpress.com.au

First published 2002
Copyright © Rose Zwi

Cover design by Deb Snibson, Modern Art Production Group
Typeset by Palmer Higgs Pty Ltd
Printed and bound by McPherson's Printing Group

National Library of Australia
cataloguing-in-publication data:

   Zwi, Rose.
   Speak the truth, laughing.

   ISBN 1 876756 21 7.

   1. Jews – Social life and customs – Fiction. 2. Social
   conflict – Fiction. I. Title.

A823.3

For Lionel and Patrick
with gratitude and affection

Acknowledgments

Some of the stories in this collection have appeared in other publications as follows:

'To Speak the Truth, Laughing' was first published in the South African literary magazine *Staffrider*, Vol.7 No.2, 1988 and was included in the following short story collections: *A Snake with Ice Water: Prison Writings by South African Women*, Ed. Barbara Schreiner, Johannesburg 1992 and *Sounding Wings: Stories from South Africa*, Eds Rosemary Gray and Stephen Finn, 1994. 'Give a Stone for Bread' was first published as 'Stones' in the Johannesburg literary magazine *Sesame*, Summer 86/87, Ed. Lionel Abrahams, and appeared in *Voices, The Quarterly Journal of the National Library of Australia*, Ed. Paul Hetherington, Winter 1991. ('Stones' won the English Academy of Southern Africa's Thomas Pringle Award for the year 1988.) A section of the novella 'House Arrest' was previously published as 'A Lonely Walk to Freedom' in *LIP from Southern African Women*, Eds Susan Brown, Isabel Hofmeyr, Susan Rosenberg, 1983 and in *Raising the Blinds: A Century of South African Women's Stories*, Ed. Annemarie Van Niekerk, 1990. The story 'Conquest of America' was first published in the Johannesburg literary journal *Quarry*, Ed. Lionel Abrahams, 1978/9. The story 'One Single to Boksburg East' won third prize in the open section of the Judah Waten Short Story Competition in 1990.

To Speak the Truth, Laughing

Anna Bronstein began paying her dues the night she spent in the cells at John Vorster Square. They had been owing since, when a child, she had seen a policeman beat up a black man in the street. She ran, sobbing, to her father's tailoring workshop.

"For this we fled the pogromists?" He got up from his old Singer machine and took her into his arms. "Will we never stop running? From one continent to another and where's it better? The goldine medina," he added bitterly, holding her close until her sobs subsided. "The golden land. For whom? Not for us and not for the schwartze. My family was right to remain in the old country. There's a time to stop running."

Anna stretched out on the grubby blanket that covered the cold stone floor of the cell. You never knew your grandfather, she wrote to her son Adam, except from photographs. You look like him; tall, thin, with the kindest brown eyes imaginable. When his family was massacred by the Nazis, his heart cracked like the floes on his shtetl's river, and his blood turned to ice. "I live," he said, "only to grieve." He did not grieve long. And before he died, wonder-tailor that he was, he sewed for me a garment of memory and guilt that could only be torn off with my flesh. But your grandmother — short, round, bespectacled like me — gave me the antidote to despair: the bittere gelechter, ironic laughter, which sustained our people through centuries of exile. It assuaged my anguish, tempered my guilt, and drove you crazy throughout your childhood. You think you can laugh at everything, you used to say, missing the underlying pain. Almost everything, I told you. One can speak the truth, laughing.

There must be a word, Anna thought, for people who compose letters which never get written or read.

Five women of varying age were sleeping on either side of her. The four nuns sat near the barred door, heads bent, in silent meditation. The rest had gathered around Joan, the student, and were talking in whispers. Three weeks ago Anna had hardly known them. She lay back, cushioning her head on her folded arms. It had been a long journey to John Vorster Square. Her parents' heritage of laughter and despair had immobilised her politically. The collective memory of her forebears, passed down by her father, had equipped Anna with an acute historical sense. This, however, was impaled on her mother's ironic laughter, a twin-edged sword: it cut through cant in both just and unjust causes, exposing not only the tyranny of despots, but also the rigidity and earnestness of the radicals and the limp humanism of the liberals. As for the blacks, they withdrew to their insulated ghettos, sending out an unambiguous message: Don't colonise our suffering, you whites; this is our struggle.

Unable to commit herself, Anna had joined movements and left movements, signed petitions and marched in protests, all of which seemed increasingly absurd to her.

"We make useless gestures while we retain our privilege and power," she said to Simon, her husband. "Tokenism, that's all it is."

"Make a revolution," Simon said without looking up from the papers he was marking, "or leave the country."

"I can do neither."

"Then don't agonise. I believe I have as much right to be in Africa as any black, provided I make a meaningful contribution."

"Like teaching Chaucer to white University students."

"There's no grand solution to the problems of Africa," Simon replied loftily. "Everyone must work out his own destiny."

Which was precisely what he did, about a year later.

In the meantime, Anna wrestled with her conscience. Like a lapsed believer on her death bed, she reverted to her former faith, trying to evade the hell-fires of hopelessness. She joined a civil rights movement, worked in their advice office, and stood on lonely vigils with placards that reflected the issues of the moment: Troops out of Namibia; No to Apartheid; Charge or Release Detainees; End Conscription; Release Mandela! The women stood alone; to be in sight of one another contravened the Riotous Assemblies Act.

But what if laws are repressive, framed to safeguard a powerful minority? Anna was reading Thoreau. "...

Law never made men a whit more just; and by means of their respect for it, even the well-disposed are daily made agents of injustice." Civil disobedience was the obvious answer.

The first test presented itself during a protest against detention without trial. The demonstration was planned for the rush hour, in the late afternoon. She was to take her stand at five o'clock, outside the University, at the Jan Smuts entrance.

As she drove through the cool, green suburbs, saturated with the smell of newly-mown grass and damp earth, Anna removed her glasses, shutting out the harsh reality of ever-higher garden walls, iron security gates, and burglar alarm plaques. She saw only a green tunnel of trees and people of indeterminate colour walking along the pavements. Observing the world through a misty gaze, however, had its hazards. Like the red traffic light she drove through because it merged with the brilliant hibiscus flowers hanging over a garden wall. Or mistaking the yellow police vans for caravans or buses. She put on her glasses. Blue-uniformed police were streaming out of the yellow vans, confronting students who had taken up the placards of the women. Bertha Egdus, from the Advice Office, was being bundled into a police van as Anna drove towards the top of the hill. "This is a legal demonstration!", she shouted, clinging to her placard — Release All Detainees. The door slammed and she was driven away.

That might've been me. Anna turned into a side-street lined with cars. No place to park. It's over, I might as well go home, no point in offering myself up for arrest at this stage. That's Simon's kind of logic, she thought, abandoning her car in a no parking area. She hurried back to Jan Smuts Avenue. The police had confiscated the remaining placards and were moving down the hill towards their vans. The students stood around in groups.

"They've arrested all the women," a student told her.

"But it's a legal demonstration," Anna said. "They weren't in sight of one another."

"Since when is legality a protection against brute force?" someone asked.

"I was supposed to take over from her, from the last one," Anna said.

"Come join us. We're going to make our own posters."

They looked so vulnerable in their jeans and sloppy shirts; pale, dry-lipped, indignant, pitting themselves against those strutting policemen in their yellow vans. Adam might have been among them. Anna longed to embrace them, protect them, send them home. Instead she found herself saying, "I've left my car in a no-park area."

"Then you'd better move it, lady," a sarcastic voice called out. "You mustn't under any circumstances break the law, even a traffic law."

Later that evening she gave Adam an edited version of the day's events. You can't tell a son everything.

Adam's call-up papers had arrived at about the same time as the black townships erupted into what the media called "unrest". And out of the dust and dry grass of the veld, names the whites had never heard of hit the headlines: Sebokeng, Bophelong, Boipatong, Tumahole, Duduza, Tsakane, Kagiso ... Burning, stoning, singing and dancing, the young ones of the townships defied the Army which had been sent in to "pacify" them, with bullets and teargas.

"There's no way I'm going into the Army," Adam had said. "Especially now. But I don't want to leave South Africa. This is where I belong."

"Leave," Anna urged. "I'll carry on with what you call The Struggle."

Adam looked at her — middle-aged, grey-haired, bespectacled, podgy. He laughed, kindly.

"First you'll have to go into training," he said, poking gently at the tyre of fat around her waist. "Twice around the golf course before breakfast. Better still, instead of breakfast."

"You think you can laugh at everything," she mocked.

"Almost everything. I had a good teacher."

Anna had paged through his army call-up papers and found a letter addressed to her and the absent Simon: "Dear Parents ... within the next few weeks your son will report for his National Service. As parents, we realise that you are concerned about his well-being ..." Adam's call-up instructions were printed in green: "In accordance with the Defence Act, 1957, you have been allotted ..."

"You could, of course, shoot off your big toe," she had said to Adam, rubbing her tingling nose. "Your paternal great-uncle Itzik did just that when he was summoned to serve in the Czar's army."

"But he wasn't a long-distance runner like me, was he?" Adam said. "My father trained me well." Simon, while he lived with them, had taken Adam with him on his daily run around the golf course. Until he ran off, in the other direction.

"True, Itzik didn't run very far. From Yaneshik to

Zhager perhaps. He never left the old country. The Czar didn't get him, but the Nazis did."

After Adam left the country, Anna's progress towards the cells had been swift and direct. She and her fellow-felons, a disparate collection of students, academics, housewives and nuns, had been shamed into action by a black woman at a meeting where Anna had read a paper on civil disobedience.

"... all our sons," Anna had said, "black, white, brown, are being drawn into a tragic conflict which cannot be resolved by sacrificing young lives ... Many of our white sons have fled rather than serve in an Army which enforces a deplorable system; many of our black sons have crossed the border for military training ... The time for making peace is now, before the land is saturated with the blood of all our sons ..."

I'd like to say there wasn't a dry eye in the audience, Anna imagined another letter to Adam. But that would be an exaggeration. There certainly was an incisive voice that cut through the rhetoric — Nomsa Modise's. "You white women talk and do nothing," she said. "Our children are shot and arrested; yours serve in the army or run away. If you really want to show solidarity with black mothers, go into the townships and tell them." So, Adam, we're going into the townships.

"If you go into the townships during the State of Emergency," Lisa, a civil rights lawyer told them, "you'll be arrested. And remember how volatile the mood is. Anything can spark off violence, even a group of harmless white women."

"When they release the dogs," a seasoned protester advised, "stand still, or they'll tear the flesh off your arms. And if there's teargas, cover your eyes and nose and walk away quietly. Don't panic."

After this invaluable advice, their numbers dropped from thirty-seven white women and three black women, to nineteen whites and three blacks. Reality, Anna discovered, was an effective extinguisher of moral ardour. Hers flickered dangerously, reviving only when she remembered her promise to Adam, Thoreau's essay on Civil Disobedience, and her father's injunction to stop running.

"Shall we pray?" Sister Imelda had asked softly before they left for the township.

Anna liked the nuns. They were pink-cheeked and serene, though Sister Caroline trembled as they joined hands to form a circle. If she, with her Connections, is so nervous, how should I feel?

"In the name of our Lord Jesus Christ," Sister Imelda began. Anna raised her head from her chest and looked around the circle. She was the only Jew among them, and an agnostic at that. A little prayer won't hurt. She lowered her head.

Dear Anon — even her prayer took the form of a letter. Please arrange a roadblock so's we'll be able to retreat with honour. And if you can't manage that, please give me strength to cope with my claustrophobia. You'll have noticed that all week I've practised incarceration in the toilet, but it's not the same; I could get out any time I liked. I don't want to disgrace myself before the Enemy and go stark staring crazy. You know how I panic in closed-in places.

Friends drove them to the township. There was no roadblock, and Anna's scepticism about the efficacy of prayer was affirmed. Her hands grew clammier and her tongue felt like sandpaper. When they were dropped off in the open lot opposite the police station, her stomach lurched and heaved. What, she wondered, if I get an attack of diarrhoea? Call off your hounds, sergeant major, I have to go to the lav. Heroic. She drew back her shoulders, raised her head and tightened her sphincter. Above all, one must retain one's dignity.

"Let's sing Nkosi Sikelela iAfrica," one of the younger women suggested. Anna wondered if she was an agent provocateur. The dogs would maul them before they said "Nkosi".

"I only know the words of God Save the Queen," Anna said.

"Perhaps a silent demonstration is better," said Debra, a very large, very black woman whom Anna had often seen at meetings. Anna moved nearer to her. Except for one or two women from the Advice Office, she hardly knew any of the others. From across the road, Lisa, their lawyer, waved reassuringly at them.

They drew their white calico bibs over their heads. Solidarity with Black Mothers, hers read. Release the Children; Troops out of the Townships, End the State of Emergency, No to Conscription, were some of the other messages written on the bibs with varying degrees of calligraphic skill. They had no strategy, no plan, only words. Linking arms in groups of five, they crossed the main road, forming a long, straggling line opposite the police station in whose cells large numbers of black children were being held.

"How long is a protest?" someone had asked at their last meeting. No one knew. Until we're chewed up by dogs, poisoned by gas, or shot dead by the riot squad, Anna thought as she watched four policemen stride out of the police station towards them. They wore jeans and floral shirts, but had holstered guns on their hips. She'd rather burst than ask to use their toilets.

"This is an illegal gathering!" the tallest one shouted.

Why, Anna wondered, gooseflesh exploding all over her body, were law-breakers thought to be hard of hearing? They'd have heard him had he whispered. He filled the place with menace as he took up an aggressive stance in the middle of the road. A weary horse dragging an ancient cart, a battered car and two bicycles came to a halt beside him. There were few other people in the street.

"You've got three minutes to disperse!" he boomed.

"Don't move," a whisper rustled down the line. They drew closer, supporting one another through linked arms. "And sit down on the pavement when time's up."

How difficult it is to break laws, Anna mused as the ferret-faced policeman shouted, "Time's up! Disperse immediately, or we'll take action."

And how scary it is to put oneself beyond its protection. A life-time's socialisation prompted her to rise and retreat when the order was given. It was with difficulty that she remained sitting in the dust. From where did the young blacks draw the courage to pit themselves against such power, to defy authority? She knew the answer, of course, but hadn't articulated it until the ungentle arm of the law yanked her up from the pavement and marched her, together with the other women, into the police station. The laws that protect us, oppress the blacks. And the blacks, as the time-worn saying insists, have nothing to lose but their chains.

The lines of battle were now drawn: she had shed her suburban anonymity and joined the transgressors, a decision she had always postponed, albeit with guilt. Adam's too young; it's not our struggle; I'm not a joiner; the blacks don't want us or need us ... Her father's heritage, finally, demanded acceptance; she had never managed to shrug it off, not with laughter and not with tears. I owe, I owe, I owe, she acknowledged, as a religious Jew smites his chest on the Day of Atonement, crying out, I have sinned, I have sinned, I have sinned! What she owed and how exactly she had sinned was not altogether clear to her, but it was a relief, finally, to stop running and take a long, hard look at what was pursuing her.

No dogs, no teargas, she continued her letter to Adam as the women were roughly propelled into the Charge Office, where black and white policemen stood behind a large wooden counter, bemused by the unusual haul. And no eager crowds cheered us on. Not that we'd planned to storm the Bastille and release the children — although that might've been a more appropriate action — but we were disappointed that only a few stragglers sauntered by, wondering no doubt, what the hell these white women — with three blacks ones in their midst — were doing in the township, so far from the green hills of home. In vain our messages fluttered over our agitated breasts; only the long-sighted could read them. And the police, of course.

In the two hours it took to enter their names and ages into a large log book, to have their bibs removed by a policewoman after they refused to do so themselves, and for whispered consultations on the phone between the station commander and Higher Authorities, the women stood around or sat on the floor, no less dusty than the pavement from which they'd been wrenched.

While they were waiting, she noticed a long-haired girl reading a dog-eared copy of *The Canterbury Tales*.

"Are you at University?" she asked her.

"Ja. At Wits. Majoring in English." She raised her book as though it was made of lead. "I hope they keep us in for a week. I've got an exam on Monday and I'm totally unprepared for it."

"Does Simon Bronstein still lecture on Chaucer?"

"Ja. He's great."

"His students always did admire him," Anna said dryly.

"Bronstein! I didn't connect. Are you related to him?"

"Only by marriage."

"Oh! I thought …"

"He was married to a younger woman?" Anna laughed. "He is now. But he does touch up his hair, you know." She leaned forward confidentially. "Light Natural Brown. I used it too. Until he ran out on us, taking the tint with him."

Some things are harder to laugh at than others.

"Us?"

"Me and our son Adam."

"Gosh! What does your son do?"

"He's a long distance runner," Anna said. She stood up and moved towards the three black women who stood in the fortress-like courtyard.

"I was so nervous," she confided to Debra. She did not know the other two women. "This is my first time," she added.

"Theirs too. And they are also shaking. Me, I've been inside for five years. Under the Terrorism Act. After 1976 I used to take the young ones over the border for training. Then someone pointed to me."

"Five years!"

"In solitary most of the time," Debra smiled grimly, passing her hand over her intricately plaited hair that formed geometric designs on her gleaming head.

"That's what scared me most, solitary," Anna said. "Weren't you panicky? I'd go mad within hours. How did you survive?"

"I was very angry. I danced and stamped my feet and sang freedom songs until my voice was hoarse and my body was tired. Then I slept."

"Do you have family, children?"

"Four daughters. Three of them are in exile. I haven't seen them for nine years. The youngest is still at school. When there's school."

"I have one son. He's been in exile for seven months. He wouldn't go to the army."

"I know. I heard you speak at that meeting. You got to be strong. Strong," Debra repeated, gripping Anna's arm firmly.

"Why did you join us?" Anna asked, rubbing her nose furiously. "You've done more than enough."

"We got to be together, man. To show them." Debra nodded contemptuously towards the counter.

Lisa the lawyer, who had been speaking to the station commander, now came over to the women.

"You're being moved to John Vorster Square," she told them.

"And the black women?" Anna asked.

"They're remaining here."

"This is a hell-hole. We must refuse to leave without them. That's what we're protesting about," Anna said.

"No point in complicating matters," Lisa said briskly. "It won't help. They keep black and white prisoners apart. I'll see you at John Vorster in about an hour or so. I'll contact your families and try for bail."

Debra laughed. Anna reddened. She was acting like a white madam only minutes after she had renounced her privileges. She walked resolutely towards the counter. Debra was right; anger held off fear.

"Excuse me," she said to the station commander who was writing into a large black book. "We're all in this together. We don't want to be separated from the black women."

He straightened up, bared his nicotine-stained teeth under his thin moustache, and wedging his hand into the back pocket of his jeans said, "What do you think this is, lady, a morning market?"

Anna walked away. A humourist. Such brilliant repartee. Our middle-class slips must be showing. But what can we expect if we turn up at the barricades with a lawyer? Rosa Luxemburgs we're not.

"Follow Sergeant Loubser out to the vans!" the station commander shouted, thumping on the wooden desk.

Anna put her arms around Debra.

"I'm sorry. I'm sorry we'll never really be together."

"Be strong," Debra said.

They were all very quiet as they got into the yellow, wire-windowed van which rattled through the township at great speed, blurring the shabby matchbox houses. The people didn't even glance at the van; it was part of their everyday lives. In a shaky voice the Chaucer student started singing "We Shall Overcome". It reminded Anna of Adam's guitar-playing days.

What did you mean, get into training, she continued her letter to Adam. There I go, all 150 pounds of me, pounding the red path between the oak trees, my cellulite dimpling in the mottled morn, getting fit for The Struggle. "Morning, morning, morning," I grunt to the joggers, the strollers and the black workers who are actually going someplace. If I'm getting so fit, why am I always so exhausted? And to what purpose? All I'm doing in The Struggle is sitting down and getting up, and moving out of police stations into wire-windowed yellow vans. For that I need to run five kilometres every day? My pulse rate, at the moment, is higher than when I'm torturing my Achilles tendons. Perhaps all one needs to keep fit is to live in a state of fear and tension. By that measure, we must be one of the healthiest nations in the world.

To Anna's relief, they were all locked into one very large cell. Its grime and dust, the seatless toilet and the headless shower, did not worry her. There was space, and through the barred door, she could look onto the corridor that ran between two rows of cells. Some cells had bars like theirs; others, the kind she had dreaded, were shut off by heavy wooden doors. None of them seemed occupied.

If I could be assured of such accommodation, she added a postscript to Adam, I'd become a full-time revolutionary, not a mere week-end protester.

"If you hear shouting or screaming during the

night," Lisa said when she visited them later that evening, "try to ignore it. The security prisoners are kept on the floor below. The Commandant has hinted that you'll all be released on bail tomorrow. You're obviously an embarrassment; they don't know how to label you. What then, Anna? You'll probably be charged with staging a gathering prohibited under the Emergency Regulations, and for entering a black residential area without a permit. If they choose to trivialise it, the Magistrate will caution then discharge you. If he wants to make an example of you, you may get 100 days or R200 fine. You'll refuse to pay the fine? Not morally guilty? That's a legitimate plea, but do remember you'll be sent to Diepkloof prison where they have only single cells, small ones," she said, looking at Anna.

The group sitting around Joan, the Chaucer student, was preparing a statement to the court: "… brutalis-ation of our youth, black and white … moral obligation to demonstrate our distress in a non-violent manner … We are one nation and demand to live together in peace …"

Words, words, words. Anna put her ear against the cold stone floor and listened intently for screams or groans. She heard only the muffled clang of an iron door, and the intermittent buzz of traffic outside. She longed to seep through the iron and concrete into cells below and shield the inmates, turn aside the blows. Adam might have been there. Or Debra and her daughters. The single light bulb cast an eerie glow on the greyness of the oil-painted walls, the floor, and the three high windows, netted and barred.

There are iron bars everywhere, she wrote to Adam.

In the suburbs they kept people out; in jail they kept people in. In our homes, freedom is an illusion; in jail, incarceration is. Not since I saw that black man lying in the gutter, bleeding, have I felt so helpless, so despairing. I know now that I shall always be on the periphery of history, unable either to redeem the past or influence the future. Only the nuns, sitting quietly in their corner, dare hope for absolution.

"This experience," the Chaucer student was saying, "has welded us into a group." Anna recoiled from her simplistic confidence. "We must plan our next action. How about a mass march on Pretoria, on the Union Buildings? We could contact trade unions, church groups, women's organisations, students ..."

Perhaps. Anna turned on to her back. Perhaps. She began her last note of the day to Adam.

How can you say I'm a poor correspondent? I communicate with you all the time. But I have a confession to make: you were right — one can't laugh at everything. Especially not at the question that has obsessed me for months now: What will I do when the flames leap across the townships into our cool green suburbs? Will I get into my running togs? Will I raise my fist and shout "Viva?" Or will I call the Fire Brigade? I don't know, Adam, I don't know. And because I don't know, my laughter leaves a bitter taste in my mouth.

One Single to Boksburg East

She could smell the chlorine long before she reached the high walls of the public swimming pool. Through the wrought-iron entrance, behind the creaking turnstile, and beyond the wall that screened the pool, she heard thuds, thumps and laughter, screams and short, sharp whistles, followed by peremptory commands. Their provenance was a mystery; she had never passed through the turnstile into the Baths.

"You're only six, you can't swim, and you haven't got a swim suit," her mother dismissed her plea to go with Nancy to the Baths.

"But Nency said ..."

"Never mind Nency Pennel. She's only twelve, she's got four brothers and sisters to look after, and can't watch you as well. When you're bigger ..."

All summer Rebecca had watched the neighbourhood children pass her house on their way to the Baths, the boys with towels around their necks, flicking one another's legs with their togs, the girls carrying tightly rolled towels under their arms.

"Becky's a Bolshie." Freddie Pennel stuck out his tongue at her. "Nency, Pency, Can't even speak prop'ly."

Nancy pulled him away. "She can't help it, she's from Russia, like the others." She gestured towards the houses of Jewish immigrant families. "I'll ask your mother again on Sunday," she promised Rebecca. "And tomorrow you can turn the rope when we skip."

Rebecca nodded eagerly. If Nancy required it, she'd turn the rope till her arm dropped off. She never laughed at her English.

"And when you're bigger," Nancy added, "you can skip as well."

The following Sunday afternoon, Rebecca waited eagerly for the Pennel siblings to appear on their veranda. Few people were out in the muggy heat. Only Uncle Ben, dressed in off-white flannels and an open-necked shirt, was cleaning his old Nash, the only car in the street. From the black-miners' compound, on the far side of the veld, the sound of drumming and chanting throbbed through the hazy air; the miners were preparing for their weekly tribal dance. Counter-pointed with the rhythmic drumming, was the unceasing crunch of the mine's stone crushers, rising and falling, soughing and sighing. Rebecca listened to her parents' fierce whispering in their darkened bedroom. She tip-toed into the room, stepping around the baby's crib at the foot of their bed.

"Go play outside, Rebecca," her mother said. Among

themselves the family spoke Yiddish. "We want to rest. The baby kept us up all night. "

"Can I …?"

"No! Just go and play."

"For a car he found money," her father said as she left the room, "but rent he can't afford. I'm sick and tired of supporting your whole family on my miserable earnings."

"Sophie's gone and Ben will also leave. He's always been generous with his car. He takes us everywhere and never asks for petrol money …"

Her father's outraged response woke the baby. Rebecca hurried into the kitchen where her grandmother was washing up the lunch dishes.

"Mamma won't let me go to the Baths."

"When you're bigger you'll go," her grandmother said.

"When I'm bigger, when I'm bigger, everything when I'm bigger …" Rebecca grumbled, returning to her vigil on the veranda.

"Ah, Beckala," Uncle Ben said, "just the person I want to see. If the car gets cleaned in time, I'll take you for a drive to Boksburg. The car polish is in the kitchen."

She ran into the kitchen, took the polish off the shelf, and brought it out to Ben.

"I'll help," she offered.

"Wipe the front bumper with this cloth. So, you want to visit Aunt Sophie? Missing her, hey? She was all yours until that horrible Simon married her and carried her off to Boksburg." He ruffled her dark curls.

Rebecca nodded, suppressing tears.

"Now you see her only when Simon feels like coming to town, or when I drive you to Boksburg."

"Before the baby was born," Rebecca sniffed, wiping her nose with the back of her hand, "mamma and pappa and me used to catch a train to Boksburg."

Two-and-a-half returns to Boksburg East, her father always said to the man at the ticket office. When I'm big, she asked him, and want to go to Boksburg by myself, what must I say to the ticket man? Vun single to Boksburg East, he replied. When he spoke English, he sounded like a stranger.

She missed Sophie. Unlike her mother, who was dark and thin and always seemed angry about something, Sophie was fair and plump, and sheltered her in her soft arms when she was in trouble with her mother. It'll pass, it'll be all right, she'd say. Your mamma's not really angry with you. She has lots of worries.

Her worries seemed to increase after the baby was born.

Don't-do-that! Her mother punctuated each word with a smack on Rebecca's arm when she leaned over the cot and touched his red, crumpled face. You must look after your little brother, not pinch him. You're the big one in the family.

If I'm so big, she wanted to say, why can't I go to the Baths with the other children? Rebecca sighed, rubbing the car less vigorously. She didn't want to hurt the baby; she wanted to be like him. But when she tried to say this, the words tightened like a knot in her throat, dissolving only with tears. Sulking again, her mother would say.

When Nancy came out of her house, Rebecca waved her damp cloth and pointed to her mother who was now on the veranda, rocking the baby in her arms. Nancy crossed the street, followed by her siblings.

"Mrs Kaplan, can Becky come to the Baths with us? I'll look after her, honest I will. She can use my tube and paddle in the baby pool. It's not deep. And it doesn't matter if she hasn't got togs, she can loan it for tuppence from the office, and it only costs tickey to go in on Sundays, but we've got season tickets," she concluded breathlessly.

For everything they've got money, except food, her mother used to comment. Meat on Sunday, and bread fried in dripping the rest of the week. You're not to eat there, do you hear Becky? It's not kosher.

Rebecca stood behind her mother tugging at her dress. "Please, please," she whispered furtively.

"Nu, all right. Take her," she said to Nancy, "but be forsichtig, uh, not let her to go in vater too muts. Vait." She went into the house for her purse. "Nem sixpence and keep penny-change for sveets."

Rebecca hugged her mother's legs, ignoring the tittering children at the gate.

"Go already," her mother responded in Yiddish, loosening Rebecca's grip with her free hand, "and take a towel from the bathroom."

"So, Beckala," Ben said, laughing, "you prefer swimming to visiting your Auntie Sophie?"

Rebecca hesitated, looking from Nancy to Ben. "Next time," she told Ben.

Rebecca stuck close to Nancy as they walked up College Street, into 11th Avenue. From here she could see the veld, the mine dumps, and the eucalypt plantation which surrounded the Blue Dam. As they turned into Dolphin Street, the smell of chlorine drifted towards them. And there, around the corner, was the swimming baths, opposite the haunted house.

"Don't look at it!" Nancy warned. "It's full of spooks. My friend Jane used to live there. Every night her mother put a basin of water in the lounge, and every morning there were bones in it. The doors creak when the spooks walk through them, and candles float in the air and blood drips down the walls. Nobody wants to live there, only the spooks. And if you look at the house, the spooks pull you in."

Rebecca drew closer to Nancy, averting her eyes from the sprawling house, so different from the semi-detached houses in the neighbourhood. It stood on a large plot, enclosed by a stone and iron fence. Many of the window panes were broken, and rusted strips of iron lace hung down from the rotting fascia boards. It was surrounded by large dark oak trees.

"And don't go past the house at night," Nancy added. "That's when spooks haunt."

Rebecca shuddered, wondering what it was spooks did when they haunted.

The wrought-iron gates of the swimming bath stood open. "Season tickets for five," Nancy said, showing the cashier her cards. "And one ticket for her and for togs," she added.

Rebecca followed Nancy through the creaking turnstile. The boys went to the left, the girls to the right, down a long open passage, on either side of which were cubicles and showers. At the end of the passage was a large room, open to the sky, in which the girls changed into their swimming togs. "Cubicles cost extra," Nancy said, as they deposited their clothes in a room with metal shelves.

Like Nancy, Rebecca put her towel around her neck and followed her outside. The sparkle of the white-tiled pool dazzled her; the mass of fair and dark heads bobbing about in the heaving water made her dizzy. Walking along the hot, red paving around the pool, she watched a boy, not much bigger than herself, climb to the top of the diving board. He stood very still for a few moments, inviting attention, then jumped up and down before throwing himself into the water, head first, his arms stretched out in front of him, rigid as her kewpie doll. She held her breath till he emerged. Shaking the water off his head, he got out of the pool, climbed onto the diving board, and repeated his performance.

Never, as she'd stood outside the swimming bath, listening to the thumping, thudding and splashing, had she imagined such an astounding spectacle.

"Here's my tube," Nancy said when they reached the children's pool which abutted on the main pool. "Keep it around your waist all the time. Nothing to be frightened of. You can stand up in the deep end. I'll be back soon."

Nancy and her family fanned out in all directions in the big pool. Freddie dived in at the shallow end, emerging on the side bordering the children's pool. He sniffed back a blob of green snot that hung from his left nostril.

"Becky's a baby, scared of water!" he called out.

She turned away, pretending not to hear. Over the wall she could see the mine dumps and the veld. The dumps looked soft and golden under the afternoon sun, dormant in the still air. In winter, a cold wind blew in from the south, whipped up the sand, and blanketed everything and everyone with fine dust. Nancy and her friends sometimes slid down the dumps on sheets of corrugated iron. Rebecca was forbidden to go there. A little black boy got swallowed up in the soft sand, her mother said, and was never found again.

When Nancy returned from her swim, she pulled Rebecca across the pool, showing her how to kick her legs.

"That's it!" she said. "Kick and move your arms like this. Practise, but keep the tyre on. I'm going for another swim."

On her third lap across the pool, Rebecca saw Freddie standing on the narrow ledge between the two pools. As she reached the deep end, he jumped in, his legs drawn under him, narrowly missing her.

"Wheeee!" he yelled. "I'm a dive bomber!"

She capsized, slid out of the tube, and sank to the bottom of the pool. There was a moment of absolute stillness as the water enclosed her: broken lines of light snaked rapidly along the tiles, bursting into short-lived rainbows. Bubbles exploded around her head.

"Mamma! Mamma!" she gasped, rising to the surface. Coughing and spluttering, she staggered towards the steps. She heard three short, sharp whistles, and saw a tall man running towards her. He lifted her out of the pool, laid her stomach-down on the hot tiles, pressing gently on her back.

"You'll be all right, little girl. And you, you're a bully," he said to Freddie who stood sniffing and shuffling at the edge of the pool. "No more swimming for you this afternoon. If you do that again, you won't be allowed into the Baths. Are you feeling better?" he asked Rebecca. She nodded mutely, a warm flow of gratitude surging through her water-logged chest. Now she knew what those short, sharp whistles meant.

"That was the supratent," Nancy explained, rubbing her down vigorously with her towel. "He looks after everything in the Baths. Shame, Becky, you got a fright, but you wouldn't of drowned. Don't say nothing to your Ma, hey. She won't let you come again if you do. And just wait till I get hold of Freddie. I'll twist his ears around his head. Hey, look, there's your Uncle Ben."

Ben stood at the top of the steps, near the entrance, shading his eyes with his hand. Rebecca dropped her towel and ran towards him.

"Beckala! You look like a drowned kitten." He laughed, smoothing down her wet hair. "Come. I'm taking everyone to Boksburg. Your mamma, pappa, the baby and Bobbe are in the car, outside the Baths. Get dressed. I'll wait for you."

Rebecca made an involuntary move towards the change room, then stopped. She looked across the pool where Nancy stood, holding her towel. Freddie sat on a bench nearby, disgraced.

"Not today," she said softly, digging her toe into a joint between the tiles.

"What are you saying, Becky? Don't you want to see Sophie? Enough for today. Get out of that funny swim suit. I'll buy you one of your own for your birthday. But now come with us."

"Next time. Today I want to be in the Baths."

"Your mother isn't going to like this," Ben said. Rebecca looked tearful. "Okay then. When you're finished, wait for us at Malka Feldman's house. We'll fetch you from there. We won't be too late." He bent down and kissed her cheek.

As Rebecca watched him walk away, she longed to cry out, wait, I'm coming! But the words knotted in her throat. Nancy was still standing at the pool, towel in hand, watching her. Rebecca ran down the steps, raising a little cough to remind Nancy that she had almost drowned.

They're in Church Street now. Rebecca visualised their progress towards Boksburg as she sat on the steps of the pool again, tube around her waist, her legs in the water. Bobbe's sitting in front with Ben, Mamma and Pappa are in the back with the baby. You're going too fast, Ben, her mother says. At twenty miles an hour? Ben replies. What do you think this is, an ox wagon? Big chochem, her father says under his breath. Everyone is looking at the baby, talking about the baby. Even Sophie won't notice her absence.

Rebecca waited at the edge of the big pool for Nancy to emerge. Her eyes still smarted and her cough, real enough now, brought a taste of chlorine to her mouth.

"I go to Boksburg now," she told Nancy.

"You can't, silly. They've left."

"I go mitten train."

Nancy shrugged. "Well, I only told your mother I'd look after you in the Baths. Give back the togs, hey."

With shivering fingers, Rebecca undressed in the empty cloak room. She put on her panties and sandals, then drew a foot through her sun-suit, tearing a hole with the buckle. Her dismay lasted only a few seconds: Sophie would fix it.

For a while she stood outside the swimming baths, listening. There it was, the thud-thump-splash, the short, sharp whistles. But the smell of chlorine no longer came from over the wall; it surged up from within. Rebecca drew a deep breath: she felt choked with knowledge. Averting her eyes from the haunted house, and with her tightly-rolled towel under her arm, she turned up the road towards Malka Feldman's house.

"Mrs Feldman," she said when her mother's compatriot opened the door looking as though she'd been wrenched from sleep, "my mother wants to lend half-a-crown."

"Today? On Sunday?" Malka Feldman looked puzzled.

Rebecca nodded. "She'll give it back tomorrow."

Malka Feldman shrugged, went into the house and returned with a half-crown.

"Thank you," Rebecca said fervently, drawing another puzzled look from the woman.

Clutching the money tightly, she walked quickly up Church Street, into Central Avenue, crossed the road carefully, and went into Mayfair Station, towards the barred window where her father always bought tickets.

"Yes?" the man said impatiently, looking up from his newspaper.

"I vant," Rebecca hesitated. "Vun single to Boksburg East," she remembered.

"First or second?"

"Second," she recalled.

"Half or full?"

"Two-and-a-half," Rebecca faltered, resentful. Her father had given her insufficient information.

"Half," the man muttered, peering over his glasses at her.

Holding her ticket and change tightly in one hand, and gripping the damp towel under her arm, Rebecca went down the steps to the platform. There were two white women near the steps, and a group of black people at the far end of the platform. She moved towards the elderly woman who looked first at her, then up the steps. Remembering the tear in her sun-suit, Rebecca turned her back to the wall.

"Where is your mummy, little girl?" she asked Rebecca.

"In Boksburg."

"Then what are you doing in Mayfair?"

"I go now to Boksburg."

"Alone?"

Rebecca nodded.

She turned to the younger woman.

"Appalling!" she said. "These new immigrants. Look at the tear in the child's sun-suit. Stay with us, little girl. We're taking the same train."

Rebecca moved closer to the woman.

"Have you got a ticket?"

Rebecca opened her fist.

"You tell your mother from me — what's your name, little girl? You tell your mother, Rebecca, that she's irresponsible. Doesn't she know what can happen?" she asked, gesturing in the direction of the blacks at the end of the platform.

Rebecca looked at her with interest, but the woman did not tell her what could happen.

"Four minutes late," she said instead as the train chuffed in, emitting short puffs of smoke. "Come," she opened a door with a large "2" on it and settled

Rebecca into a corner of the green leather seat. "I'll tell you when to get off."

"Mayfair, Braamfontein, Park Station, Doornfontein, Jeppe," Rebecca recited a list of stations as her father did when they went to Boksburg. "George Goch, Denver, Tooronga …" she continued breathlessly until she reached Boksburg East.

"The child's a freak," the woman said to her companion.

Rebecca smiled, pleased with herself. She had forgotten one or two stations, but the old lady didn't seem to notice. She turned to the window, watching the yellow mine dumps flash by; she waved to the black miners who were standing around the concession stores and compounds in their colourful blankets; and where the railway line ran parallel to the road, she waved at the passing cars. Then she closed her eyes and felt the shadows of the trees and poles press darkly against her eyelids. "Terrattacha, terrattacha, terrattacha," she sang softly, in unison with the train. It was much nicer travelling alone; her mother always said, shhh when she started to sing. The old lady did not even look at her; she was reading a book.

The train stopped at every station, letting people off, taking others on, and soon the carriage was so crowded, that the old lady sat right next to her. When the conductor came into the compartment, Rebecca gave him her squashed, damp ticket.

"Nice little girl you've got there, Ma'am," he said to the woman. "Looks like a little gypsy."

Gypsy, freak; she must remember to tell Ben the new words she learned today.

As they approached Boksburg East, the woman spoke to her again.

"Do you live far from the station?"

"Mine aunty is in Market Street," she said. "Number 149."

"And your mother?"

"Mit mine aunty."

"Appalling," the woman said. "You tell your mother from me that I have a good mind to report her to Child Welfare. Never mind," she said when Rebecca repeated "child velfa" very carefully. "Just be careful. Goodbye," she added more kindly, opening the door for Rebecca.

Rebecca walked quickly down Market Street, joyfully anticipating the family's surprise.

"I had enough at the swimming baths," she will say as she comes onto the veranda where they'll be drinking tea, "so I came to Boksburg by train. I'm big now."

"Zulig!" Ben will laugh, ruffling her hair.

"Ziessie!" Sophie will enfold her in her soft arms.

"Well, she is the big one in the family," her mother will say. "I even let her go to the swimming baths today. What can babies do? Nothing but lie in their cots and mess in their napkins."

"You're my clever girl." Her father puts his arms around her.

"What do you expect?" Bobbe asks Simon who is standing at the door. "That she should sit in Mayfair and wait for you to bring Sophie to visit her?"

Rebecca saw Ben's car as she approached the house, but no one was sitting on the veranda. They must be having tea in the dining room. Still clutching her damp towel under her arm, and holding the change in her clammy fist, she opened the screen door. As it fell back with a little tap, she heard Sophie call, "Who's there?"

Rebecca walked into the dining room and stood in the doorway, smiling. There was a moment of silence, as though she were under water again, then everybody started talking and shouting at once.

"It's all right, it's all right," Sophie said softly after her mother had hit her so hard, that she not only dropped the rolled up towel and spilt the change; she also had red finger marks on her arm. "First your mother was worried because you'd stayed behind, then she realised you'd come all that way yourself and worried about what could've happened to you. Don't cry so, my baby. You're breaking your heart and mine. Just go up to her and say you're sorry, and promise not to do it again."

Her mother was changing the baby in the bathroom. Rebecca stood quietly in the doorway, holding back the whimpers that rose from her heaving chest. As her mother opened the baby's napkin, Rebecca saw a curry-coloured mess all over the towelling square and over his dimpled bottom. Now he's going to get it. Rebecca brought her hand fearfully to her mouth to suppress another sob.

"Good boy," her mother said softly, removing the dirty napkin from under him and wiping him deftly with cotton wool. "That's what's been worrying you all night and all day. Now you'll have a comfortable journey home, my little babbala."

Rebecca rushed out of the house, into the hot car. Even Sophie's pleas to come inside for supper could not dislodge her from a corner on the back seat. She fell asleep after a while, and only woke when her father lifted her onto his lap as Ben started up the car.

They drove up Market Street, turned right, then went under the railway bridge, past the prison where bad people were sent, her mother once told her, people who had broken the law. Rebecca never knew exactly what it was that they had broken, but wondered if there were any little girls under those roofs, the tips of which were visible above the high stone walls. She shivered, and her father covered her with the blanket Sophie had thrust into the car before they left.

The journey home was long and tiring. Rebecca watched the mine dumps darken and merge against the inky sky until only the slanting rows of cocopan lights were visible up the slopes. The windows of the concession stores were dimly-lit. The miners had departed; the music had stopped, and the dancing was over. The stone crushers roared and crunched as they drove by, then faded into the silence of the night. And every now and again, they overtook a horse-drawn night cart, the stench from which was overwhelming. Rebecca nuzzled against her father's chest.

Between the heads of Uncle Ben and her grandmother, Rebecca watched the lights of Johannesburg flicker in the all-encompassing blackness of the night.

"Nearly home," her father said.

That night, Rebecca dreamed she stood at the top of the diving board, with the pool on one side and the haunted house on the other. She walked to the edge, looking down at the shimmering water. She drew back, afraid to dive. Go, go! Freddie shouted, leaping up the rungs of the diving board towards her. She turned to the haunted house and saw candles floating through the broken windows.

Damp with fear, she wrenched herself from sleep, listening to Mrs Pennel's rooster crow. After a while she fell into an uneasy sleep again. She was a baby, lying in her mother's arms. They were travelling down a dark road in Ben's car, and as they overtook a night cart, it swerved into them, spilling its load on the car. Her mother's face floated above her, smiling. Good girl, she said as she changed her napkin.

Rebecca woke to the rhythm of the stamp mills in the distance, mistaking it for the beating of her heart. The dream faded, but the smell of the night cart persisted. Slowly she lowered her hand, moving it cautiously into her pajama pants. It came away warm and sticky. Moaning softly, she lay very still, her throat closing up. Mamma, she called quietly. Mamma!

Carved in Stone

Esther changes into her working clothes and goes out to her studio, a wooden shed at the bottom of the garden, on the verge of the bush. Here, tulip magnolia, azalea and tibouchina bushes weave a tapestry of colour against the sombre greens of the grevillia, eucalypts and tea trees: Australian natives mingling with exotics with a blithe disregard for botanic purity.

"Look to the plants, ye zealots, among whom Rachel is queen," Esther murmurs as she looks around the garden which she and Samuel had cultivated with love. On her work bench is a half-completed sculpture in tawny sandstone of a mother and child — perhaps a father and child — her gift for Anne and Gideon on the birth of their son. Had Rachel sculpted, religion permitting, she might have done one of a father sacrificing his son to God.

She has had yet another rancorous argument with her sister. Earlier that morning she had phoned to tell Rachel that at last she was a grandmother. Mother and child are well, she said, and Gideon was there throughout the birth, doing a couvade ... What's a couvade? It's Gideon's way of saying he played a supportive role during Anne's labour ... Don't be silly, Rachel. He wasn't performing primitive rites. Anthropologists study pre-literate societies, they don't go native, as you put it ... Well yes, I suppose he could've studied his own culture more thoroughly, but even rabbis' sons marry out of the faith ... I didn't ask about circumcision. That's their decision ... What d'you mean I pussyfoot around my children? Samuel didn't either ... He did not regard himself too smart to adhere to his own tribal loyalties. He was a rational, warm, human being who had respect for other people's beliefs, and felt free to pursue his own ... Of course we had friends of different race and religion ... On the contrary, I think we set a good example ... Deborah? She's still working at the Children's Hospital ... She doesn't want to go into private practice ...

Sure she loves children; she just doesn't want any of her own ... Perhaps she thinks there are enough children in this sick, over-populated world ... Feline over-population? She's got two cats, not twenty, and those she red-crossed, as she puts it, from the street ... Stop referring to him as her de facto; he's got a name. Michael, remember? You've known him for seven years ... He's a lapsed Catholic ... There is a difference ... For goodness sake, Rachel, I phone to give you good news, and you turn it into a religious rant ... I'm not over-excited. I'm just sick of your self-satisfied moralising ... I leave for New Zealand next Monday ..."

Nothing's changed. At fifty-eight, Rachel is still playing big sister. On her ninth birthday, she'd been given an illustrated book of stories from the Old Testament. When Rachel read her the story of Abraham, Esther, four years younger, had wept. Why did he have to send Hagar and Ishmael into the desert with only a jug of water and some bread? Stupid girl, Rachel said, God was going to make Ishmael into a great nation, it says so in the book. And why did God tell him to sacrifice his son? Esther shuddered every time she saw the illustration of the white-bearded Patriarch, knife in hand, standing over Isaac who was tethered to kindling wood on an altar. You don't understand anything, do you? Rachel said irritably. He was testing Abraham's faith.

Rachel's own faith has never wavered. For which God has blessed her with three obedient daughters who married within the faith, and produced eleven grandchildren.

Anne is at the airport to meet her. "I needed a break," she tells Esther as she wheels the trolley to the car. "And Gideon, besotted father that he is, was happy to be left with Alexander for a while."

Alexander. Such a heroic name. Gideon could've named him after his own father. Esther pulls herself up. Rachel's poison has seeped into her bloodstream.

Anne grunts as she lifts the suitcase into the boot of the car. "What on earth have got in the case, Esther? Rocks?"

"I've been knitting for the b…, for Alexander."

"Come off it. You can't knit."

"Well, it's my substitute for knitting."

"It's a sculpture! Wonderful!"

"Tell me about Alexander."

Anne is pale, her eyelids are droopy, but she glows as she speaks of the baby. "He's got a tiny, crumpled face, fuzzy black hair, and perfect little hands and feet, long skinny limbs. Gideon says he resembles your late husband. He loved him very much. I'm sorry I never knew him."

"Samuel's students also loved him …" Esther's voice falters.

"Gideon admires your work too, Esther. He says you make stone speak."

"You should hear my sister on that subject. She's sure I've sold out to strange gods."

"Is she very religious?"

"Depends on your definition of religion. She's unquestioning, observant, concerned with ritual."

Anne is quiet for a while. "I want to talk to you about, well, religion. I had offered to convert, if it was important to Gideon. He said as a child he'd asked if you believed in God. Samuel said no, and gave him a Child's Guide to Darwin, illustrated. You said you'd like to believe, but couldn't. In later years Gideon appreciated your honesty, but at the time he felt like an outsider at the Jewish school you sent him to."

"I'm reaping," she murmurs.

"Pardon?" Anne leans towards her.

"It's in keeping," Esther says, "with our ideas at the time. We wanted him to know what his traditions were so that he could chose when he was older. A cop out, I suppose."

"Have you changed your mind, over the years?"

"Even Samuel made the odd compromise."

"And you?"

"Why do you ask, Anne?"

"Things get complicated when you have children. At school, everyone is something, Jewish, Christian, Hindu, whatever. There are festivals to celebrate, fasts to observe. Although I'm not religious, I'd be happy ... But Gideon says he's not going to bring religion into our home. He hated the atmosphere in your sister's house. He's grateful, now, that you and Samuel allowed him to think freely." She hesitates. "So we've decided not to have Alexander circumcised."

Esther is glad of the dark. She starts to speak, but the words catch in her throat.

"You're upset," Anne says.

Keeping her voice steady, Esther says, "Even Samuel couldn't withstand that when Gideon was born. But we didn't have a religious ceremony. A doctor did it. Post-Holocaust, Samuel had said, apologetically. Millions of innocents martyred for what they were, for their beliefs, their customs. Always the anthropologist, he'd joked, feebly, that even cannibalism is understandable in its cultural context ..."

"There are dangers of haemorrhaging, you know. And previous ideas of hygiene aren't proven ..."

Esther can no longer hold back the suppressed emotion of the past week. She weeps silently, her head turned away from Anne.

"Esther! I'm so sorry. Gideon should've discussed it with you."

Esther grasps her extended hand.

"I shouldn't cast gloom at such a joyful time," she says. "I'm so happy about Alexander. Let's not say any more about it."

"Indeed we shall, all three of us. It's your grandchild, after all."

"Tell me about your house. After your tiny apartment, it must be good to have space. And a garden."

"It's a wonderful find. A client, for whom I'm designing a house, put me on to it. It belongs to his sister who's in the throes of a divorce. He's letting us have it at a low rental for a year, with an option to buy. It's a bit run down but comfortable, one of six houses on a cliff top overlooking the bay. It's magic. The garden runs along the edge of the cliff, closed off by a baby-proof fence."

"Wonderful view, low rental, an option to buy. Where's the catch?" Esther asks, relieved at the change of subject.

"The house is built on disputed territory. The land is part of a very old Maori settlement. Nothing remains of the stockaded fortress, the pa, except a grassed-over area. And white settlers built the houses alongside the pa."

"Territory. Always territory."

Anne explains that during World War II, buildings, bunkers and observation posts had been erected on the cliff. The Maoris were now demanding the return of the land for their own housing, and have moved into some of the buildings. But they're up against the vested interests of property developers.

"How do you feel, living on disputed territory?" Esther asks.

"Uncomfortable. Gideon has spoken to the squatters, but they're deeply suspicious of all pakeha, white settlers, especially those actually living on their land. Gideon's put together historical evidence for the Maoris, supporting their claims."

"If they succeed, you may have to leave the house."

"Gideon may win their trust. If not, we'll move. Here's our driveway. The beach is only about a hundred metres away. Listen to the waves crashing against the cliffs. It's high tide. The beach is narrow. You can only walk on it at low tide. Come this way, Esther, to the front garden. The moon's about to rise."

Anne leads her over the spongy lawn towards the cliff's edge. Only the stars differentiate the elements in the all-embracing dark. In silence she and Anne watch the coppery light brighten in the east. A crescent moon rises slowly from behind an island, laying a bridge of scaly light across the bay, linking island with mainland, dimming the stars with its brilliance.

"Imagine the ancestors in their ghostly boats," Anne shivers, "rowing silently down that bridge of light, their oars dipping in the waves, coming to reclaim their heritage." She laughs. "See what happens when you haven't had enough sleep?"

"You'll have to propitiate the ancestors."

"Which ones? Come inside, Esther, you must be tired and cold. There's a cool breeze blowing up. The weather bureau forecasts thunder storms."

Gideon embraces Esther warmly. He leads her to the lounge where the baby is sleeping in a wicker bassinet.

"He likes Bach," Gideon says, turning down the volume. "Especially the Goldenberg Variations. He looks like Dad, doesn't he?"

"Uncannily so. Oh look, he's grimacing, puckering up his mouth. Is he due for a feed?"

Anne points to the damp spots over her breasts. "He is indeed. Pick him up, Esther. Get to know your grandson."

As she lifts him out of the bassinet and her lips find

the soft, vulnerable centre of his head, Esther knows she could never give him up to the knife, surgical or ritual. She remembers the nights of questioning and soul-searching before Gideon's circumcision. It had not helped bind him to his ancestors.

While Anne feeds Alexander, Gideon shows her around the house.

"A state of shabby disrepair," he comments as he leads her from room to room. "We'll renovate when we have more money. That's why I married an architect. I'm not sure why she married an impecunious social anthropologist."

"So's you can smoke a pipe of peace, or whatever the local custom is, with the Maoris, propitiate their ancestors, and be allowed to stay on this wonderful cliff with them."

"Anne's told you. What else did she say?"

"Everything relevant."

"And how do you feel about it?"

"I'm sad he'll grow up cut off from his traditions."

"We'll send him to you. You can fill him in on tribal history. I consider myself a citizen of the world, not a member of any particular culture. I'm looking for the beliefs and practices which bind people together, not those that separate them."

"Spoken like your father's son."

Gideon looks at her uncertainly. She smiles at him.

We succeeded, Samuel. Beyond our wildest dreams. Take pride in our creation: an independent, free-thinking man who assimilated all the lessons of his childhood. And he looks so distinguished, with the first grey hairs at his temple, a scattering in his bushy black beard. A little like Darwin himself. Or am I thinking of

Marx? All nineteenth century intellectuals and thinkers look alike to me.

Esther listens gravely as Gideon speaks about the universality of creation myths, ritual as appeasement to the vengeful gods ...

"Does the Holocaust mean anything to you?" she interrupts.

"A great deal. And I see it repeated in the tragedies in places like Cambodia, Mai Ly, Rwanda, the tribal wars in Somalia and other parts of Africa, the agony of Yugoslavia. Nothing approaches the scale and savagery of the Holocaust. But that doesn't mean I want to spend my life re-enacting rituals which are not meaningful to me. The most I can hope for is to reach some understanding of the human condition."

"A modest objective."

He looks at her sharply, then turns to the sculpture which Anne has placed on the mantelpiece. "This mother and child is very subtle. It could be a father and child."

"I'm pleased you noticed." Esther stretches up and kisses him on the cheek.

During the two weeks Esther spent with them, the subject of the circumcision was never raised again. She helped with the cooking, and cared for Alexander while Anne caught up with sleep. She watched Gideon bath the baby, and was moved by his tenderness. All the facets of Alexander's development fascinated her. The grasping of a finger indicated unusual strength; every windy grimace was interpreted as a smile; the furrowed brow accompanying bowel movements, presaged great intellect. His parents modestly disclaimed genius, but after consulting books on baby rearing and development, agreed he was advanced for his age. Esther had never felt so close to Gideon and Anne; Alexander had brought them together. Tradition was relegated a back seat to love. As she took him from Anne, his mouth damp with milk, his lips blistered from sucking, her heart ached for his vulnerability. Had she known any rites, primitive or civilised, which might ensure his safety, she would have practiced them gladly. She spent every available hour with him. Only when he slept, and if it coincided with low tide, did she walk on the beach.

It was a curved, narrow beach, with dun-coloured sand, and dark, weathered rocks lying at right angles to the sea. The sandstone cliffs rose steeply from the beach, capped by pohutukawa trees that leaned precariously over the edge, as though preparing for flight.

In pools between the rocks, Esther found pebbles milled by the waves, the wind and the sand, into round and ovoid forms, with grooves and holes that created a multitude of strange forms and images. No human hand has shaped these, she thinks as she squats beside a rock pool, drawing out the pebbles, turning them over in her hand, then replacing them: it seems sacrilege to remove them.

Gideon is delighted when she describes her feelings. "You're on the same wave-length as the Maori," he says. "They also feel mystical powers at work, something that can't be explained by science. They believe certain stones and tree are tipua, that they contain the souls of dead people, and they therefore become sacred, tapu, the most powerful institution of Maori life. If you transgress and pollute the tapu of a tipua — are you still with me? — dire retribution awaits you.

Poets and artists should work with pre-literate cultures, not so-called scientists who descend on them with a bagful of theories, then proceed to fit them into the proverbial Procrustean bed."

Only once had she encountered any of the Maori squatters who lived on the far side of the cliff. She was walking along the beach one morning when she saw three women, their skirts tucked up, wading through the water, searching among the rocks. Occasionally they dropped something into a basket which stood on one of the rocks. As she drew nearer, they straightened up and returned her greeting. Two women were middle-aged, broadly built, with warm brown eyes set in smooth, unlined faces. Their black hair was rolled up in a bun. The young girl was slim, and wore her hair loose. She smiled shyly at Esther when she asked what they were collecting. Sea eggs, very delicious, she said, holding out the basket to Esther. Esther thanked her and said she'd recently eaten breakfast. The women laughed, then turned back to their work. She never saw them again.

On the day before her departure, towards sunset, Esther takes her last walk on the beach. Black-backed gulls glide on the rising breeze, and the sea rocks gently as the tide goes out. She walks along the gravelly sand, scampering over the slippery rocks and stopping from time to time to look at the seamless slate-grey sea and sky. The horizon is defined only by a ship sailing out to sea. As the clouds move in, the cries of the gulls slip away on the wind, and an unnatural stillness engulfs her. An eternity passes before the waves break again, and the gulls mewl feebly as they fly overhead. Shaken, she sits down on a rock and stares at the pebbles in a rock pool.

The dying light falls on a pebble at her feet. She picks it up, glances at it, then throws it down with a quick jerk of her wrist. She tries to walk away, but is incapable of movement. Forcing herself to pick up the pebble again, she looks at it closely. It resembles a death's head or a tragedy mask, she cannot decide which. One eye is round, the other is oblong, grooved, and the wide beak-like mouth seems to emit a silent scream; her ears ring with it. There is one nostril in a blunted nose, and its skull is concave, with indentations and holes down the back. Gripping it firmly in her hand, she returns to the house. She will probe its meaning later; now she needs to return to her own world.

Gideon comes home late that evening. He has been to a meeting with the squatters whose petition for housing has been turned down.

"They say the Government does not dispute that this is Maori land. My historical research confirms this," Gideon says. "But they refuse to build housing for them. The property developers, it seems, are too powerful. The squatters have refused an alternative offer. They want to live on their ancestral land."

"What will you do, Gideon?"

"I don't know. I haven't exactly won their trust. I do have a vested interest, after all. It's all very complicated."

"Move," Esther urges, surprised at the warmth of her response. "It's a wonderful place, but do you feel you belong?"

"I suppose not."

Esther holds Alexander close, passing her lips gently over his furry head. "Move," she repeats softly.

Gideon is unusually quiet all evening. They sit in the lounge, listening to music, while the waves crash against the cliffs, roof tiles rattle in the wind, and sheet lightning flashes across the inky sky, followed by claps of distant thunder.

"We should put up curtains," Anne says when they go to bed. "We're too exposed to the elements. But the view is so beautiful."

Esther lies awake a long time, listening to the gathering storm. Once she imagines Alexander is crying, and walks quietly into the lounge. He is asleep in his bassinet, breathing softly. Eventually she falls into a restless sleep. She is walking along the beach, watching clouds race across a purple sky. As she clambers over the slippery rocks, the tide comes in, pinning her against the cliff. Her heart beating wildly, she begins to climb, grasping at a root, a ledge, an outcrop of rock. She climbs faster, her hands raw and bleeding, when she hears the cry of a baby. With a desperate effort, she pulls herself over the top of the cliff. The crying grows louder. She runs into the lounge and pulls the blanket off the bassinet. A death's head lies on the pillow, its beaked, toothless mouth open, emitting a long, drawn-out shriek.

Esther tears herself out of the nightmare and lies back panting, her body bathed in sweat. The storm is at its peak. A loud clap of thunder is followed by a long rumble, as though rocks are falling into a ravine.

The stone head! She feels for it in the drawer of her bedside table. Grasping it tightly, she hurries through the house into the garden. Blinded by lightning and whipped by the rain, she runs towards the edge of the cliff.

"Take it, it's yours!" she shouts into the storm, throwing the pebble over the cliff.

Back in the house she rubs herself down, and changes into dry night clothes. Shivering violently, she gets into bed, and as the storm dies down, she falls into a heavy sleep. The ringing of a telephone wakes her as the first light of dawn presses against the window.

"Incredible!" she hears Gideon exclaim. "A whole section of the cliff, taking the fence with it? ... No other damage ... Thank goodness ... I didn't hear a thing. I'll be down in a few minutes."

Esther comes out of her room as Gideon hurries down the passage, pulling on a heavy sweater.

"I heard," she tells him. "Gideon, it's a sign, it's a sign!"

He looks at her, incredulous.

"You really believe it," he says, putting his arms around her. "Go back to sleep, mother, and give it no further thought. Wind, wave and water action, you know. A perfectly natural phenomenon."

Indigenous Man

The shadow of the car lengthens as the sun, fierce and low, ignites the dry veld with its last rays. Get to the hills before dark, Christine had warned. It's often misty and the road to the farm is rutted and rocky after the turn-off. My father's letting everything revert to nature.

With minutes to sunset, Jeanne has not yet reached the hills. The red-tinged veld, with occasional ploughed-up mealie fields, stretches away to the horizon. Red-roofed farm houses and mud-daubed huts of farm labourers, stand isolated, unadorned, in the long grass, without a tree in sight. She slows down as she approaches yet another rural town with a cemetery, a police station and a black township on its outskirts. Cylindrical wheat silos tower over austere churches and dull-fronted shops, and houses with iron lacing line streets wide enough to turn a span of oxen. She is grateful for the Depression that had driven her forebears out of the heart of these flatlands into the city.

The sun goes down, draining light and colour from the sky. Changing gears as the ascent into the hills begins, she enters a different world: damp, misty, an east wind driving low clouds across strange rock formations, weathered and lichen-covered. The land on either side of the road is fenced off, and an occasional signpost names farms she cannot see through the mist: Eagle's Eyrie, Farfields, Pine Lake. The farms on the parched plains had been called Sandspruit, Onverwacht, Vergelegen.

The road dips, and she emerges from the mist. All around are hills, and in the valleys between them, metallic-hued dams glow in the twilight. Watch out for the signpost, Christine had said. My father makes sure he doesn't have many visitors. A narrow white arrow with Newman written small, points to a deeply-rutted road with sharp stones jutting through the red soil.

Her ageing Volkswagen shudders violently as a rock grazes its undercarriage. Straddling the road, with two wheels on the grassy verge and two wheels on the centre hump, she drives with intense concentration, seeing nothing but the ochre road that winds around a low hill. One more bend and Newman's house appears in the feverish light that still glimmers in the west. It is a long, wooden structure with a pitched roof. From its chimney, a thin wisp of smoke dissolves into the thickening dusk.

On the covered veranda which runs the length of the house, stands a bearded man, smoking a pipe. He is dressed in khaki and wears a wide-brimmed hat. From a distance he looks like any other farmer she has ever seen. But as she approaches — he remains motionless, his left foot resting on the wooden railing — she senses a stillness in him which evokes dark forests and steaming earth.

Ralph Newman had been watching the dying light fade from the regenerating forest that stretches along the valley on both sides of the stream. Each year the forest creeps imperceptibly towards the crest of the hill, on the far side of which the land drops away to the plains. Gradually it is re-establishing hegemony over the swarded slopes that had long been denuded of their natural bush by fire and grazing cattle. Twenty-six years ago, when he bought the farm, he had found a narrow fringe of riverine shrub on the banks of the stream. After he sold off the cattle, stopped the burning, and forbade the use of indigenous trees and shrubs for firewood or medicine, the bracken once again unfurled its furry, spiralled crowns and, together with other ferns and mosses, the original forest floor was recreated under the shaggy grey-green branches of the honey-scented sagewood, the blue-green pittosporum, and other trees and shrubs that had lain dormant or deformed during the long years of the fires.

Newman watches the young woman emerge from her battered Volkswagen. In jeans and loose shirts, their long hair hanging down their backs, this generation of women all look alike. My friend, Christine had said over the crackling line two nights ago, is doing research in your area. She needs to stay over one night. What research, he asked, but never heard her reply. Oh, let her come, he said finally, exasperated. She won't impinge on your privacy, Christine laughed. I've warned her that my father's a crusty old hermit.

"I'm Jeanne le Roux," the stranger says, holding out her hand.

"Newman," he says gruffly.

"I hope I'm not intruding. Christine said it'd be all right to stay overnight. I'm visiting other farms in this area ..."

"I'm not a farmer and this isn't a farm. Nor am I geared for visitors. There's a stone cottage," he points towards the back of the house, "where Christine stays when she comes. She likes her privacy. Like me."

"Christine sends love. She's been very busy ..."

"Don't apologise. She doesn't. She hates the farm. Not happy unless there's concrete under her feet and telephone wires overhead. Trees give her hayfever. I'll take you to the cottage. Willem's lit the combustion stove for hot water. No electricity. Only a candle and matches."

My father's a man of few words, Christine had said. Solitude's done nothing for his charm.

The cottage stands under the ridge of the hill. It's a square, tin-roofed dwelling, the sort of house an ungifted child might draw. The rooms are sparsely furnished, with a plain deal table and four chairs in the front room, and an iron bedstead and pedestal in the bedroom. The third room is locked. A small kitchen, empty except for a combustion stove, adjoins the toilet and bathroom. The walls are roughly plastered and white-washed, and the floor is laid with concrete tiles. The smell of mould, woodfire and something undefinable, clings to the walls and the ceiling.

"We eat in an hour." Newman puts down the candle and matches on the table and walks out of the cottage.

Through the small, uncurtained window, Christine

sees heavy clouds drifting over the hill. Distant thunder rumbles through the row of eucalypts that stand like sentinels on the ridge. She turns back the blankets; the white sheets are stiffly starched. Like they used to be on her grandparents' farm. Stretching out on the creaky bed, weary and overwhelmed by the strangeness of her surroundings, she falls into a deep sleep.

Newman clambers over the rocky ground towards his house. Strangers. He is constantly afflicted with strangers. What does one say to them, do with them? This one reminds him of Christine, and when he thinks of Christine, he feels a pang of loneliness. When she comes, she laughs and talks and teases. Long after she is gone, her voice reverberates through the house, surprising him. She certainly does not take after him. Nor after Myrtle, who had been a quiet woman. While Myrtle was alive, Christine had visited regularly. Now she comes only at Christmas and at Easter. As though these festivals mean anything to him. Just as well. They get on better when they're apart. Had Simon lived ... Three years older than Christine, he had died at the age of five. It was then that Newman had sold his farm on the plains and moved into the hills.

He stops, draws in a sharp breath, and frowns. At the far end of the forest, near the dam, a curl of smoke rises above the treetops. Furtive smoke, from a secret fire. Damn the man; he has returned. Is there no getting rid of him? He will speak to Willem immediately. This time they will drive him right across the border, into Swaziland. Angry, uneasy, Newman sets off for Willem's huts, at the back of the house.

Bathed and refreshed, Jeanne makes her way along

the overgrown path that leads to Newman's house. The lounge is lit by several hurricane lamps. One stands on a table set for two on a threadbare, clean cloth. Another is on a yellow-wood coffee table in front of the fireplace, on either side of which are two shabby arm chairs and a small couch. At the back of the room is a narrow bed covered with a dark blue bedspread. The third lamp stands on a desk, behind which is a glass-fronted bookcase.

After my mother died, Christine had told her, my father closed off all the rooms except the kitchen, the bathroom and the living room, where he does most of his living, such as it is. He's obsessed with redressing man's abuse of nature. And when he isn't walking through his regenerating forest, he's reading books about indigenous trees, shrubs and mosses.

Jeanne glances at the books on his desk: Morphology of Vascular Plants, Lower Groups; Cryptogamic Botany; The Medicinal and Poisonous Plants of Southern and East Africa; a pile of journals whose titles are obscured by a notebook. Scattered all over the desk are notes written on odd scraps of paper, in a small, tight handwriting. Jeanne moves away from the desk when the kitchen door opens. Newman walks into the room carrying a battered tray with a bottle of whisky, ice, water and two glasses.

"It gets cold here at night," he says. "We stopped lighting fires only a week ago." He pours a large tot of whisky into each glass. "Water? Ice?" He doesn't ask if she drinks whisky.

"Ice, please. It's another world up here. It was so hot and dry down in the veld."

"There'll be rain tonight," Newman says, listening

to the intermittent thunder that rolls over the desolate plains. "Up here we don't need much rain. Mostly gentleman farmers with trout dams. Or pine forests. Tax dodgers. Weekenders, whose managers burn the grass and plant pines or eucalypts that suck the rivers dry. Not to speak of Australian wattles that take over our indigenous forests. Intruders. No respect for man, beast or bush."

Newman sinks into an armchair, motioning Jeanne to take the other.

He stares into the night, saying little until he has downed his third whisky. Then he speaks jerkily, disjointedly, as though his thoughts are flowing along a subterranean river on a dark, secret course, surfacing briefly with a sentence or a phrase, then descending again into its silent depths. At first Jeanne tries to connect one sentence to another, but soon realises he is not addressing her. Perhaps, during his years of solitude, he has lost the ability to distinguish thought from speech. She sits back, her cheeks tense from smiling politely, and nods whenever it seems appropriate.

The smell of cool, damp earth comes in through the doors which open onto the veranda. From time to time, sheet lightning flickers across enormous clouds, illuminating the hills and the valley.

"Thunderbird, shepherd of heaven indeed." Newman frowns. "Willem believes everything that man says. And now he's back, with the first thunderstorms."

Should've sent him packing immediately. Wild-eyed, smelling of sweat and khaki weed. No job here, I told him. Not a proper farm. Just two cows for milk, and a vegetable garden. Only Willem and his family live here. Can I sleep here, only this night, the man had pleaded. Too cold and too dark to leave now.

"Only tonight. Tomorrow you must be gone. No job here."

Jeanne sits up, startled. "That's all I intend staying," she begins. He is not addressing her. He is looking out into the night. She sits on the edge of her chair, clutching her empty glass.

"Another drink?" Newman takes the glass from her. "Lizzie isn't ready with the supper." He sniffs the air. "Rain. Coming nearer." He sinks again into the subterranean regions.

I should've sent him away. Next morning he was sitting on the kitchen steps, hunched up in those foul rags, his eyes red, his skin grey. All I was short of, a corpse on my land. Willem, tell him he can't stay here. Tell him only you and your family live here, because your father worked for me and I've known you since you were a boy. The intruder turns his red eyes on Willem and speaks in a voice like muted thunder, pointing towards the hills, beyond the forest. He says his ancestors are buried on this land, Willem said. He can show you. When the white man took away the land, his people had to work on the mines. Tell him, Willem, that my wife and son are also buried on this land. It wasn't true. Willem, even more territorial than I am and no friend to strangers, just hung his head and said nothing. He was clearly intimidated by this stranger. He is a shepherd of the skies, Willem said. He makes medicine against the lightning. He hunts the thunderbird. Tell him, Willem, that he must go. Give him some food and my checked shirt, and tell him to go. But Willem was not about to mess with the shepherd of the skies who hunts the thunderbird and whose ancestors were buried on my land.

"The intruder's ancestors," Newman explains. Jeanne looks puzzled.

Willem took him in, gave him some old clothes, and found a place for him in that maze of mud huts he's built over the years. I rarely go there. That's Willem's territory. Must respect a man's territory. That's where the kitchen gardens are, where all our food is grown.

"I'm a vegetarian," he tells Jeanne. "I've slaughtered enough animals in my years of farming. Ah, here's Lizzie with supper."

A buxom black woman with a scarf tied low over her forehead comes into the room carrying two bowls of steaming food on a tray. She sets it down, then walks out, without raising her eyes.

"Christine tells me you're doing research." Newman dishes up the curried vegetables and rice. "What on?"

"It's for a Ph.D in history. About land rights, or lack of land rights, under apartheid. I'm interviewing people in this area about the time the Nationalist Government ceded a chunk of long-disputed land to Swaziland, to rid itself of part of its 'black problem'. Black people hadn't been consulted at all. Everything seems to revolve around territory, doesn't it?"

"You've got to respect a man's land." Damn the woman. She doesn't understand a thing. To have come now, just as the so-called shepherd of the skies returns. "Nothing's changed, new South Africa or old South Africa. This is my land. He belongs there, over the border."

Willem and his family had been in awe of the man. They believed this land belonged to his ancestors, that we were aliens, from the plains. I was angry, frustrated, but I know how strong their superstitions are, and I need Willem. He can't live here, near the house, I told Willem. He can have the hut next to the dam, and he can get a weekly ration of mealie meal. But if he doesn't remain on his side of the land, if he disturbs anything in the forest, I'll kick him out. And the rest of you had better stay away from him. He's a stranger, from another nation.

"If you speak Swazi, you're a Swazi," Newman says emphatically.

"It's not that simple. These people had been living here for generations. They'd put down roots ..."

"Not indigenous, don't belong here," Newman mutters.

The intruder's presence had discomfitted him. He often bumped into him in the forest, wandering about, mumbling to himself, coughing that racking cough. But he was always polite, deferential even. Until that night.

"Not indigenous," he repeats.

"Who is indigenous?" Jeanne asks. "My forebears were Huguenots from France; yours probably came from England."

"Scotland," he says sharply.

"People become naturalised. Even trees and plants ..."

"Nonsense! Introduce wattles and pines and eucalypts, and they take over the forest, kill indigenous trees."

Ignorant girl. What does she know of the power of trees? The stranger knows. The bark had been stripped off the pepper-bark tree near the dam. The man had either dried and ground the red, bitter bark for snuff, or chewed it to clear his chest, or inhaled its smoke.

Leaves had been scattered around a sagewood, the *Buddleia salvifolia*, which he'd probably used as a decoction for his cough. And he was ruining the *Catha edulia* in the forest, the Bushman's tea shrub. He knows it's a narcotic drug, but doesn't realise it can cause insanity, coma, even death.

"I was very angry," Newman says, wishing the girl wouldn't look so startled every time he speaks. "Tell him, Willem, I said, that he is not to tamper with the trees of the forest."

But Willem was no longer telling the stranger anything. He himself had begun grinding the roots of the sour-plum, the *Ximenia caffra*, which he mixed with cowdung, then smeared it onto the floors of his huts, to ward off the witches. The stranger was disrupting everyone's life.

"We have to send him back to his own country," Newman tells Jeanne.

"This is their own country." Jeanne speaks passionately, irritated by Newman's idiosyncratic use of the third person singular. Is this his way of minimising the problem?

"He coughed a lot," Newman says, staring out at the lightning which is drawing closer.

Which was why he had stripped the pepper-bark tree. But it was the *Catha edulis* that was driving him mad. He had rushed into the kitchen that night, brandishing an axe, shouting that the graves of his ancestors had been desecrated. Lizzie had run away. It took Willem, his brother and me half-an-hour to overpower him. We tied him up, put him into the van, and drove him to the border. By that time he had calmed down. I gave him some money and let him loose. He disappeared into the night. And now he's back. Vengeance? Sanctuary? Who knows.

Jeanne stands up. "I'd better get to bed. I have to make an early start tomorrow morning."

"Where will you be going?" he asks, his spirits lifting at the thought of her departure.

"I'll move around the rural areas and interview farmers and their workers about that ugly period in our history."

"Don't get shot. The other farmers may not be as amiable as I am." A faint smile quivers in his beard. It does not reach his eyes which look distracted, sad. "I'll walk with you to the cottage," he says.

"Really, it's not necessary."

Newman does not reply. He leads the way to the cottage, his head bent against the wind which is coming up. The first large drops splatter down as forked lightning rips through the heavy clouds, sinking its shafts into the surrounding hills. The thunder, nearer now, reverberates through the valley.

"Shepherd of the heavens indeed," he mutters.

He lights the candle, closes all the windows of the cottage, locks the back door, then places a key in the front door.

"Be sure to lock the front door after I leave. Goodnight."

Jeanne's head aches. She'd have liked to see the regenerating forest. Christine, no nature lover, had raved about the tree ferns, the flowering shrubs, the clear stream, the cascades. But communication with Newman was impossible. He seemed to be in the throes of an unending interior monologue. And he kept staring into the night, as though expecting ghosts to walk in from the gloom.

She gets into bed and blows out the candle. The dark is almost palpable. Through the uncurtained window, she watches spears of lightning stab into the eucalypts on the hill which bend and sway in the wind like demented dervishes. Another flash of lightning, thunderclaps that rattle the windows, then abysmal darkness. She dozes off from time to time, but cannot fall asleep. Once she imagines footsteps pounding up the path; another time, a sound like steel on glass. Or is it the branch of a tree scraping against the iron roof? She lies very still, tense, her eyes shut, conscious of every breath she takes. She wants to open a window, but is afraid to get out of bed: she feels she is being watched.

She stares at the window but sees only the dark night pressing against it. A sudden flash of lightning lights up a dark, ravaged face on which all the agony of Africa seems etched: sunken eyes, the whites rolling over in pain, a broad nose with quivering nostrils, and a mouth wide open in a silent scream. A scream rings out. She does not know whether it is his or hers. She shuts her eyes tightly. When she opens them, the face is gone. Moments later a lone figure flickers briefly on the ridge, arms outstretched, as though challenging the heavens to strike him down.

"Sleep well?" Newman asks when Jeanne walks onto the veranda next morning, gritty-eyed. There are two black men with Newman, carrying heavy sticks. One of them has a rope looped over his arm. They look sullen, uneasy.

"Very stormy night." She adopts his laconic tone. "Tell me, why did you spare those eucalypts on the ridge? Not indigenous, you know."

"Don't look for consistency in human behaviour," Newman says quietly. "Besides, they're far from the forest."

She looks towards the forest. A wisp of smoke is floating above the tree-tops, dissolving almost instantly into the clear air.

Newman too is looking at the forest, frowning. "Breakfast's in the living room," he says.

"No breakfast for me, thank you. Lizzie brought me coffee early this morning. I must go. I have a heavy day ahead."

He walks with her to the car. On the way, he moves towards a eucalypt sapling growing in the tall grass.

"Don't!" she cries out involuntarily. "It's so far from the forest!"

"You don't understand." He crushes the sapling under his heel.

She reverses the car and starts her descent to the main road. Rain water rushes down the road, deepening the gulleys, washing away the soil. Soon the road will become impassable and his isolation will be complete. But Newman does not need people; they complicate life. How is one to know who is native and who is not? Plants and animals are easier to classify. When she reaches the bend in the road, she looks back. He is standing on the veranda, talking earnestly to the black men, pointing to the forest.

Laugh, Kookaburra

His approach, as always, sets off the neighbourhood dogs. Through the kitchen window, she watches him move down the empty lot behind the house with a long, bounding stride. The golden Labrador from a house abutting on the plot, is first to raise the alarm. In summer he lazes under a tree, in winter he follows the sun. But when his territory is invaded, domesticity sheds like bark from a eucalypt. He rushes to the wire fence, fangs bared, gnashing and snarling, barking and baying. Like the dogs of the hunters.

Tosca, the Maltese poodle from the house on the left, tears around the verandah, yapping and yowling, scratching at the railing which separates her from the intruder. The afternoon's tranquillity is shattered by the barking of unseen dogs. Only Mattie, from the house on the right, part fox terrier, part something larger, is conflicted. She stifles a growl, barks half-heartedly, then retreats to her cubby-hole under the verandah steps.

"Doesn't know if she's Arthur or Martha, dog or dingo," her neighbour Janet had told her when she first witnessed the canine hysteria. "Mattie practically brought him up, you see, but when the other dogs go berserk, her doghood stirs."

The previous autumn, Janet said, fishermen had seen a pack of dingoes scavenging at the far end of the beach. A few months later, they spotted two pups on the sand dunes. As they approached, the pups disappeared into the bush in response to their mother's agitated, cough-like barks. Soon afterwards, on an early morning walk with Mattie, Janet saw a pup stagger out of the bush. He was black, with white paws and a white tail tip. His ribs stood out against his mangy fur, and his eyes were gummy. The pack must have moved on, leaving the runt behind. Mattie walked towards him, emitting soft sounds. The pup watched her nervously for a while, then slid on his belly towards her, ears back, tail down. Mattie licked him, and the pup rolled over, whimpering. But as Janet moved towards him, he stumbled back into the bush.

She returned later with some ground meat and a container of water. The pup emerged, sniffed cautiously at the food, and keeping a wary eye on Janet, gulped down the meat. The next day he was waiting for them on the verge of the bush. After he had eaten, Janet released Mattie, who bounded over to him with a joyful yelp.

In the following weeks, the pup's eyes cleared and his fur began to shine. He leapt into the surf with Mattie, chased sticks, and romped with her on the beach. At first, he shied away from Janet, but eventually allowed her to approach, to pat him, and even took food from her hand. Soon he was following them home.

"The kids love him. They call him Dingy. Not very imaginative, but none of us is a whiz with words," Janet said. "I know you shouldn't feed wild things, but if I hadn't, he'd have died. And look what a magnificent creature he is. The neighbours hate him. He'll take our cats and dogs, they say. Just what you'd expect from them. He's a wild thing, isn't he? And if it moves, shoot it."

"I thought Australians felt an empathy with loners, outlaws, underdogs," she said. After fifty years in the country, she still spoke of Australians in the third person.

"Ever heard of the bounty? A hundred years ago a dead dingo was worth five shillings. The price increased over the years, and the Dingo Board went bust."

She was surprised by her urge to touch Dingy, to look into his eyes. She'd always been afraid of dogs: the peasants' dogs that barked at them in the countryside; the hunters' dogs that tracked down fugitives; the militia's dogs that herded them to the grave.

"You don't like dogs, do you?" Janet said one day as she drew back involuntarily at Mattie's approach. "But it's different with Dingy. I've seen the way you look at him."

"He's such an elegant animal. Lean, long-legged, with those white markings on his throat, chest and legs. Wolf-like ..."

Every night the peasant had released them from their living grave. Long enough to lie in, high enough to sit under, the trench had once been a store for potatoes. When she and her mother escaped from the death march to the mass grave, the peasant had taken them in. He enlarged the trench in the centre of his hut, and punched airholes in its iron lid. He was an honourable man, much indebted to her father. He let them out only at night; the penalty for harbouring Jews was death. She and her mother crawled out into the icy air which tore at their throats, seared their lungs. Walking backwards, they covered their footprints in the snow. With icy fingers, they picked lice from their hair and shook earth from their cerements. Engulfed by darkness, they heard the howl of the wolves, echoing their fear, loneliness, cold and hunger. But the wolves, at least, were free. Even now, so many years later, far from the forests and the snow and the huntsmens' dogs, the smell of the trench cleaves to her nostrils. Back in the hut, they slept next to the wall oven, stretching their limbs, warming their bones. At first light, when they climbed back into the trench, she was overwhelmed by terror and panic. She wanted to flee, to run with the wolves ...

"Let's say I have an affinity with wild things," she said.

"You write books in English, speak it so well ..." Janet hesitated.

"But have such a heavy accent?" She laughed. "Accents are difficult to shed, but cannot be discerned in the written word. I studied English and literature at school, in Europe, but used it only when I came to Australia, after World War II."

"What kind of books do you write?"

"Depressing ones," she said. "You wouldn't want to read them. But they have to be written."

"Will you ever write about Australia?"

"When I know what the kookaburra's laughing about."

"Got to fix tea for the kids," Janet said, and never asked again.

She and Tadek had once slept over in Eagle's Eyrie on a return trip from the north. We should buy a cottage here, Tadek had said, marvelling at the beauty of the pale gold beach which stretched northwards in a gentle crescent, fringed by a cerulean sea, and at the islands that lay like great whales off the mainland. When he died, six months later, she sold their apartment in Bondi, moved into a small flat in Surry Hills, and bought a clapboard cottage at Eagle's Eyrie. At first she drove up from Sydney at two-monthly intervals, staying a week at a time. Now she comes more frequently, for increasingly longer periods. After an early morning walk, followed by a swim on warm days, she spends the morning writing. In the afternoon she either reads or goes for long rides on the bicycle she bought from the Cycology Shop in Kurrawong Street.

She loves their humour, their playfulness with language. So different from her own people's, which is sharp, with a bitter edge. She responds to greetings in the street, and when she hasn't spoken to anyone all day, or needs to disperse the dark clouds from her mind, she initiates conversations. "Taking your fish for a walk?" she once asked a man who was dragging a trussed-up dead fish across the beach to entice blood worms out of the sand. "No," he replied, quick as a skink. "Teaching him to swim."

She is an outsider, by choice and by exclusion: she is regarded as an eccentric foreigner who keeps to herself. She knows, from the weekly local paper, that there's an active social life in the town, but has refused Janet's offer to induct her into it. She doesn't play bridge or golf; doesn't like bingo or the pokies, and is useless at handicrafts, baking and cooking. She's never been a joiner, not of political parties, nor of good-works organisations. She can no more be a Rotary Lioness, than a Zioness. She is obsessed with the imperative of history: to bear witness. A small price for survival.

"You could teach creative writing at the U3A lectures," Janet once suggested.

"Writing's a penance, not a creative activity," she replied. "I hack words out of rock. Yes, I was married, to a resistance fighter who saved my life. But no, I never had children, lucky unborn creatures."

The only person she spends time with is Janet, who lives next door with her two teenage children. My ex-husband mines opals at Lightning Ridge, Janet told her, but all he's ever dug up are undersized fragments which he sells to jewellers for inlay work. He's still looking for the Big One. She supports herself and her children by working as a receptionist for the local doctor, hence knows what's happening in town. It was through Janet's network of friends that she learned a petition was being drawn up for the removal of Dingy from town.

Janet phoned her immediately. "Come as soon as you can," Janet said. "They've donned their white hoods. Laura's dachshund's missing, and two feathertail gliders have been killed. Dingy's been accused and sentenced, without trial. I've phoned the National Parks and

Wildlife Service and asked them to take him to a nature reserve. We only do that with pure dingoes, they said. He's pure dingo, I insisted, down to the white spot on the tail. No black dingoes in your area, they said. They'll class him as feral dog, and the catcher will get him. He'll be gassed. There'll be no dissenting voices. We must go to the Council. I'll offer to adopt him, to get a licence, anything."

"I'll be there early tomorrow morning," she promised.

She left for Eagle's Eyrie at sunrise, racing against the dog-catcher. She usually enjoyed the three-hour journey, but today it seemed endless. She drove distractedly along the freeway which cuts through great slabs of striated sandstone, barely glancing at the eucalypt-covered hills that stretch away to the coast. This beauty, she once told Tadek, dies in the eye: no connecting tissue to the heart. Give me the forests of my childhood, the birch, pine and fir forests — birjoza, sasnai, yolke, she chanted — and the oak, lime and beech forests. All pitted with mass graves, he replied. There's no going back.

The ubiquitous eucalypt and the anglo-celtic population had seemed so bland, so boring. Miles and miles of dull, ash-green trees, unchanging with season; a laid-back people, sequestered by distance from a world of menace. Then she began noticing the cenotaphs in every town and village; heard tales of the Depression, saw Aborigines in city slums. And seasonal change, she discovered, was carried not in the foliage, but in the trunks and branches of the eucalypt. With the onset of spring, they shed grey bark and brown bark, and burst out of their green anonymity into brilliant shades of amber, ochre, and red-brown; orange, copper and salmon-pink; white-grey and yellow-green, pink-grey and lime green. Connective links were established between eye and heart.

She drove straight to the surgery. A brief talk with Janet reassured her, for the moment. The dog-catcher came on Thursdays. That gave them a few days in which to register their protest at Dingy's deportation, and arrange for a reprieve until he was legally "adopted".

All day she's been listening for the rattle of the dog-catcher's van. They'll take us by surprise, she told Janet; they won't wait for Thursday. She had not felt such fear since she and her mother had huddled together in the forest, listening for the bark of the huntsmen's dogs, for the crackle of dry twigs. She is therefore delighted to see Dingy run across the empty plot towards house, and jump over the low wooden fence into her back yard. Safe; he's reached den. The barking dies away. He sits quietly on the small patch of lawn, front legs crossed, looking expectantly towards the house. She wants to rush out and embrace him, but will wait till dark. She doesn't want to provoke the neighbours. They know she feeds him when she comes to the cottage, but have never expressed their disapproval openly, as they have with Janet. They're a little wary of you, Janet told her, but there've been mutterings about that woman with the limp and the funny accent. The witch and her familiar, she had responded wryly.

She had been delighted when Dingy first accepted food from her hand. Soon afterwards he allowed her to approach him and stroke him, even when she was not dispensing food. Francesca of Assissi, guardian angel of wild things. But self-deprecation cannot mask her pleasure in Dingy's friendship. She hopes she can save him from the gas chamber.

Later that evening, as she sits by the fire listening to music, she is overwhelmed by unease. Dingy is on the front lawn, howling at the moon which intermittently breaks through the clouds. Unlike the wolves, he is not completely wild. But he retains enough of the truly wild to be rejected by *Canis familiaris*, the barking, yelping, yapping domestic dogs. They feel threatened by him, as do their owners. A wild thing. Yet how would he fare in the wild? Discarded as a pup, will he be accepted full-grown with the smell of human contact all over him? He howls out his loneliness, his dislocation. She had recognised him immediately: the scapegoat of the ages, reincarnated to replay his eternal role, this time in a small coastal town.

She longs to bring him in, out of the cold, to sit with her at the fire. Janet is in her lounge with Mattie at her feet. She herself has a book on her lap, a disk in the player. Cosy, warm, protected from the wind which joins with Dingy's howls, while the branches of the eucalypt claw at the iron roof.

In the trench, under the iron lid with the airholes, they had heard the whispered conversation between the peasant and his brother-in-law: ... hunters with dogs are searching for fugitives ... you must get rid of them ... no, you can't just let them go ... they'll betray you under torture ... you'll be shot ... move the table, turn wall oven over the trench, come to town for Easter ... no alternative.

Before the iron lid was lifted off the trench that night, she and her mother had hidden their few possessions in the folds of their clothing. We're going to town for Easter, the peasant told them. He was pale, distressed, and could not meet their eyes. I'll leave you food and drink, he said. Her mother kissed his hands, wetting them with tears. Through knee-high snow they fled to a little wood her father, a timber merchant, had sold to a group of woodworkers. They were permitted to hide in the forest, but were not taken into their homes. She and her mother built a temporary shelter from fallen branches, and remained in the forest till the snow began to melt. The cold and damp took their toll: swollen joints, fever, coughs were the least of their troubles. The snap of dry twigs, the crackle of a gun, the barking of dogs, paralysed them with fear: there was no place to hide. If not for the food left by the woodcutters at the edge of the forest, they'd have died of hunger. When, in early spring, the wood was encircled by the militia and their dogs, the woodcutters led them into a neighbouring forest.

Where did you meet your husband? Janet once asked her. In a forest, she replied, together with a group of resistance fighters. Was any of your family with you? Only my mother. And your mother …? Killed in the crossfire, she said, between the anti-fascists and the local militia.

She goes to the window. Dingy is sitting in the same place, with his head between his front paws. She will take him back to the city … To her one-bedroom flat? And what of her town neighbours and their dogs? No. She'll remain in Eagle's Eyrie; she cannot give him up to the dog-catcher. But what of her own life, the few friends she has, her subscriptions to Musica Viva, the symphony concerts? Can she lock up a creature used to his freedom in a city flat? What alternative does she have? Turn the wall oven over him?

After a restless night, she wakes to the yodelling of the magpies and the maniacal laughter of the kookaburras. She goes to the window. Janet is leaving for her morning walk, with Mattie and Dingy in tow. An elegant animal indeed: long-legged, with white markings on throat, chest and legs. Oblivious of his fate, he walks behind Janet, his white-tipped tail held high.

She knows why the kookaburra is laughing.

Conquest of America

From her tenth floor hotel room, through the open window that looked as if it hadn't been cleaned since the Depression, Iris heard the first tentative notes of a violin tuning up. The tremulous notes lingered momentarily in the heavy evening air, only to be drowned out by the roar of Broadway traffic, punctuated by police or ambulance sirens, she didn't know which. Depends on whether the population was being decimated by muggings or by coronaries.

She had been in New York ten days. Soon after her arrival in New York she had taken a cab to her agent's Fifth Avenue offices, enlarged and refurbished since her previous visit to New York.

"The literary market is depressed," he complained. "You'd be better served by a new agent who could begin with the freshness and enthusiasm needed to push your books."

"Are you axing me?" she asked lightly. New York

must be lousy with agents; publishers were her problem.

"Good heavens no!" He handed her a list of ten literary agents. "The best in town," he said.

His chins shook with earnestness as he assured her that her writing was good, excellent in part. But there was a limited market for that sort of thing.

"Let's meet for coffee one day," he said as a taxi skidded to a halt beside them. On her previous visit, he had taken her to dinner.

"Let's." She accepted the phantom invitation.

"You must know lots of people in New York," he stated.

"Not a soul," she replied.

"Lovely." He bundled her into the taxi. "Keep in touch and let me know how it goes. Contact the publishers MacNeill and Schmulowitz. They gave you the best rejections."

She withdrew against the hot upholstery from his sibilant, spluttering speech. The taxi drew away, leaving him on the sidewalk, wiping his brow. She could not forgive him his relief. "What are you doing in New York?" the taxi driver asked her. She told him, succinctly. "You never know," he said. "There was this Australian dame who wrote a book about birds or thorn trees and she made a million."

Thin straggling violin notes rose again above the noise of traffic. He's having difficulty warming up tonight, Iris thought as she took off her reading glasses and rubbed her tired eyes.

All over New York people were sitting in cafes and restaurants, laughing, talking, perhaps agonising. But in company. There were days when she approached any friendly-looking stranger, usually old or female, and asked to be directed to some street or another. Just to establish temporary contact with another human being. Have a good day, she'd be bidden after directions were given. They made it sound as though it were her democratic due.

Time for immersion-element tea. She filled her Woolworth's mug with water, placed the element into it, and slipped its nether end into the shaver plug above the wash basin. When it boiled, she took out an Earl Grey tea bag from her box of twenties, and dipped it into the mug; American tea was tasteless. Stepping into her sandals — the tackiness of the worn carpet made her feet curl with revulsion — she placed the mug on the writing table next to a Baby Ruth chocolate bar. Chocolate was comforting, even if it wasn't Cadbury's. She glanced at the half-finished letter headed "Conquest of America — Part Three." Some conquest. Her family would appreciate the irony. Of course it was more important to write than to be published. Yet ...

She returned to the window, watching the crowds pour out of the theatre on 46th Street, part of whose facade was visible from where she stood. The violinist, whom she could not see, was playing that sunrise-sunset song from Fiddler on the Roof. She imagined the theatre-goers digging into pocket or purse for a coin to throw into his open violin case, or hurrying by with averted eyes. Yesterday she had seen a girl in jeans on Fifth Avenue, playing a Bach violin study. "Help Pay Fees of Juilliard Music Student," her poster demanded. And they gave; they even applauded.

Iris's violinist played apologetically, badly. As a child he might've practised only the melodic bits. Or perhaps he'd foundered on the rocks of ambition, with insufficient talent to match. Self pity, drink, lost pride, and finally a stand on 46th Street. His candied repertoire suggest this. Or perhaps he was just a bum.

The cars started up in the parking lot, revving and hooting. Against the orchestrated cacophony of city sounds, the violinist played the opening bars of the Mendelsohn violin concerto. After battling with an intricate passage, he took refuge in the slow movement. Her heart ached for his flat notes. How much easier to hear dissonance in music than in literature. She shut the window and returned to the writing table.

Opening her Michelin, she turned to the chapter headed "New York and Literature." With a pang she glanced through the list of writers who had written in and about New York, among them Scott Fitzgerald and Thomas Wolf. Both had been nurtured by Maxwell Perkins. Every writer deserves a Maxwell Perkins.

After ten days in New York, she had not only failed to unearth a Perkins; she hadn't even found an agent. After she left Sheldon that afternoon, she had phoned every literary agent on his list. "My name is Iris Wycroft," she began. "I'm an unpublished novelist in search of an agent. I'm in New York for a short time and wondered if you'd care to see a sample of my writing."

One agent said he ran a small establishment and could not handle any more business. Another asked for a reading fee of fifty dollars. A third questioned her about the locale of her novels and sounded doubtful when she told him. A few suggested she bring in a chapter or two. Not interested; won't sell; not our sort of thing; too remote for the American public; well-written but. She felt humiliated by the agents' rejections. She hadn't even made it to first base, as they say in the States.

Her last two contacts were the publishers whose rejections had impressed Sheldon. They remembered her novels, they told her in neutral tones when she phoned, and would be delighted and charmed, respectively, to meet her. Delighted. Charmed. Not merely pleased. She ignored the neutral tones and allowed herself to hope again.

The interview with MacNeill took place one afternoon about five days after her arrival in New York. At that time she was still staying in the quiet hotel on East 58th Street, into which Sheldon had booked her. "You must live in a relatively safe area, especially as you're travelling on your own," he had written. "Be in by sunset," the porter told her as he showed her to her room. "Lock, bolt and chain the door. Don't open up for anyone. And don't use the subway," he warned, pocketing the tip. "Keep away from Greenwich Village and don't walk in Central Park. There are hippies and druggies who'd mug their grandmothers for a quarter."

The heat wave which was to engulf Manhattan a day or two later had not yet set in. On her way to her appointment with MacNeill, she had walked through the streets with a light step; hope had given the sidewalks spring. Everyone looked well-groomed and sophisticated, just like the advertisements in glossy journals. Americans have open faces, she generalised happily as she bought a pretzel from a vendor. Have a good day, he said as she walked away, vibrating with the vitality of the streets.

The forty-storey building bore the name of the

publishing company for whom MacNeill worked. With assets like that, they can take a risk on me. Thus far she'd been caught up in a literary catch twenty-two. No one wanted to publish an unknown writer, and a writer couldn't get known until she was published. All she needed was a break.

Larry MacNeill was good-looking in an off-beat way. His dark hair was longer than that of the business people in the streets, and his teeth had an un-American yellow tinge. But his dark-lashed blue eyes were soft and sensitive. He would understand.

"It's like this," he said after telling her she wrote well but. "I have to show a profit, and let's face it, there's no money in this sort of thing. If I'm not to lose my credibility with the directors. Sex, violence, perversion sells. Have you tried it?"

The pace is fast in America. No time to finish sentences.

"... can only accept the occasional book on literary merit alone," he was saying. "I'm pushing Jasmine Laquer. Heard of her?" He reached to the bookshelf behind him. "Read it," he urged earnestly. "It's very good. Sensitive. But by signing up more of this, I'd destroy the specialness I've tried to create around Jasmine."

Iris looked at the book. On the dust cover was a picture of a delicate-looking young woman.

"Haven't you a place for another flower in your stable?" she asked fighting down the desperation in her voice. It had a dissonant tone, like a badly-tuned violin.

"It's the specialness, you see," he said, averting his eyes.

On her return to the hotel on East 58th street, she

counted her travellers' cheques. In terms of her flight concession, she had to remain in New York another five days. If she stayed on at this hotel, she could not afford food, let alone theatre. Her travel agent had given her the name of a cheap hotel on West 47th Street. The area's a bit dicey, he'd warned, but the hotel rate is reasonable, for New York. She packed her bag and took a taxi to West 47th Street.

Her room, at the back of the hotel, was long and narrow and the furnishings evoked dusty, second-hand sales rooms. The air conditioner didn't work, so she forced open the window and looked on to 46th Street where she saw part of the facade of a theatre. She turned back the shabby bed cover and sighed with relief: the sheets were clean. And there were clean towels in the bathroom. Liveable.

She peeled back the mud-brown blanket and lay reading Jasmine Laquer's book, failing to discover its specialness. That was the first time she heard the violinist tuning up. Acting on impulse, she dressed and hurried out of the hotel. By the time she reached 46th Street, the theatre crowds had dispersed, the parking lot was empty, and the violinist had disappeared. She joined the motley crowd on Broadway and was surprised she did not feel nervous. Perhaps New Yorkers exaggerated the violence and the muggings; Broadway look safe enough to her. Darkness obscured the litter and the dirt, the tawdriness of the advertisements. She hardly noticed the pimps distributing hand bills for sex shows, the disoriented drug users. During the day Broadway aroused unsuspected evangelistic depths in her, and she understood the breast-beaters' cries of Sodom and Gomorrah! Fire and

Brimstone! Sea of Iniquity! Behind the desperate pursuit of pleasure, she smelled decay. It was not vitality she had felt in the streets; it was the frenzied convulsions of a dying culture.

Yet good plays were being produced off Broadway. Baryshnikov was dancing at the Met; art galleries flourished, and books without gratuitous violence, sex or horror were still being written. No thanks to Larry MacNeill.

Emboldened by her venture into the streets, she decided to use the subway the following day, to walk through Central Park on her way to the Metropolitan Museum and spend the day at the Village on Saturday. She wanted to see the real New York. She would not sit around in her grotty hotel room waiting for rejections.

In addition to the usual tourist activities — the boat trip around Manhattan, the view from Empire State building, visits to the Rockefeller Centre and the United Nations — she walked in the Village and on the Lower East Side and took a ferry ride to Ellis Island and the Statue of Liberty. She spoke to people in the subways and in the parks, and became friendly with the Jewish owner of Kelly's and Kennedy's, the delicatessen store from which she bought the bagels, cream cheese, tomatoes and yoghurt that constituted her daily diet. She wondered if she knew the proprietor well enough to ask: Which one are you, Kelly or Kennedy?

On her last weekend, she went to the Ninth Street Neighbourhood Festival. She walked through the crowded street, tasting exotic food prepared by the various ethnic groups who lived there. This was more like her original idea of America: the racial mix, the melting pot. The tenements behind the gay street stalls, of course, told the other side of the story. A couple of well-dressed black men stood beside her at the Hawaiian stall, watching the preparation of something that looked like a bamboo shoot rissole.

"Tempting," one of the men said to the pretty young cook, "but tell me, where can I get an ordinary hot dog?"

She shrugged contemptuously. "Ask Gimbels where Macy's is," she replied.

Although she moved about at night, she never stayed out late, nor walked in the darker side-streets. She was usually back in her hotel room in time to hear her violinist tune up. She did not try to find him again, allowing him his mystery.

On the night before her interview with Langley Schmulowitz, she allowed herself to hope again, to fantasise. After a rejection by him, her powers of hope and imagination would have shrivelled irrevocably. She bathed, made her tea, ate her Baby Ruth, then watched the news on the temperamental television set.

Schmulowitz would be tall and lean, with shortish greying hair. Once she had fantasised about blond Viking-like men with chiselled faces and green eyes. Or dark Slavic types with soulful black eyes. Schmulowitz was definitely grey. He had burning, angry eyes under slanted bushy brows, untouched by grey; angry at compromise, burning with literary zeal. She wondered, as she walked into his meticulously kept office, what colour the hair on his chest was.

"Black," he said, motioning her to a chair, without looking up from the manuscript he was slashing mercilessly.

When he finally looked up, she felt herself dissolve

in the heat of his penetrating gaze. She would have fled had she not seen the involuntary movement of his Adam's apple. He, too, was affected by this meeting.

"Iris Wycroft," he said in a firm voice. "I was expecting someone quite different. Dry, withheld, ascetic, with a touch of puritanical modesty, if your writing is anything to go by. You're a full-blooded woman, why don't you write like one?" he demanded angrily.

"I beg your pardon." Iris got up from her chair.

"Don't beg. Demand. Sit down and listen, woman. You're afraid to hate, love or criticise strongly. Life is raw, brutal and uncompromising. Say so. Don't contort yourself into knots trying to be fair or kind or understanding. Your men and women must love and hate and act on it, not squirm and pine and luxuriate in their spindly consciences."

He got up suddenly, covering the distance between them with a few strides.

"What you need is to be good and truly fucked."

She gasped and pushed him off, furious.

"You crude beast! Is vile language your idea of how bull-flooded, full-blooded, men and women should act?"

"No. That was shock therapy. This is how they should act," he said, taking her into his arms and bringing his mouth down on hers with a firmness and tenderness that sent shocks of ecstacy through her body. She put her arms around his neck and felt him quail under the ardour of her kisses. They separated shakily.

"Where are you staying?" he asked.

She told him.

"That dump! You're moving in with me."

"Won't your wife mind?"

"Don't be smart," he frowned. "I'm divorced. How long are you here for?"

"Another two days."

"Make it two months."

"I can't. My concession ... I'm running out of money ..."

"The firm will deduct it from your royalties."

"You're going to publish me?"

"Not until you and I have worked night and day on your novels. They need an infusion of real life and they're going to get it. You can do it. You have talent, ability. We'll make a writer of you yet."

Coward, Iris told her image in the mirror. You pulled out of that one before you had to construct a real love scene. But you did manage a four-letter word. With a little practice, you could write crap with the worst of them.

Next afternoon, before her interview with the real Langley Schmulowitz, she took more care than usual with her appearance. He kept her waiting for only five minutes before the secretary ushered her into the small, untidy office at the end of the corridor.

He was short, rotund and boyish, with light brown hair, a sort of Simon and Garfunkel, whichever it was that had the frizzy hair.

"Iris Wycroft," he said. "I was expecting someone completely different. A little older perhaps. Do sit down. Just throw my squash racquet off the chair. Terrible heat, eh? But you must be used to it where you come from."

For the next ten minutes they discussed the laid-back lifestyle in her country.

"Ah yes, your novels," he said finally. "They have a bitter-sweet quality, good descriptions, evoke atmosphere and the people come alive. But the relationships lack sexual tension. And if you'll pardon me, the books all need a stronger story line. Yes, oh dear yes, as our friend Henry James has said, a novel tells a story."

"E.M. Forster," she corrected, but he wasn't listening.

"Well-written but. Not the sort of thing. You must realise. Not the reading public for it. Oh dear, what is it, Ms Wycroft? You've suddenly gone so pale."

"Nothing, nothing." She fought off waves of nausea. "There seems to be a broken record in my head, playing the same phrases over and over again. Haven't been sleeping well. Not used to living in an air-conditioned cash register."

He stood up in alarm.

"Where are you staying?" he asked.

"At the ..." Suddenly her mind went blank. "I've forgotten. Don't be alarmed. It'll pass. It happens to me often. I mean, it's just the heat and all that ..."

She stood up. He walked her to the lift, his arms outstretched, helpless.

"Perhaps I should call a cab. Or better still, I'll phone Sheldon Landsman. He must know where you're staying."

Iris drew herself up.

"Sheldon Landsman no longer works for me," she said. Then she remembered the name of her hotel.

"Temporarily slipped my mind," she said, stepping into the lift.

As the door shut on his astonished face, her lips trembled. She'd have to hold back her tears until she got back to her hotel room. This was hardly the place to let go.

Only two more days. She couldn't wait to get out of New York. The sidewalks had grown hard underfoot, the faces were closed and uncaring. Have a good day sounded like a curse. Iris switched off the reading lamp and went to close the window. She preferred the heat to the noise. The violinist was playing his last piece for the evening: Humoureque. She heard the staccato rhythm of the music recede into the distance as he walked away to catch a later show at some other theatre.

Love, Sara

LONDON, 5 September 1973

Dear Dvora,

I've temporarily shed my roles of wife-mother-daughter, in-law and out-law, and I'm enjoying my one-ness. I'm staying with Pat. You remember her. We taught school together until she was arrested, jailed, released, then house-arrested before she left for London on a one way ticket. She lives in the East End and has a tough teaching job for which Judo is a more appropriate qualification than an MA in English literature. Tiny flat, peeling plaster, rusted bath, but warm hospitality. We talk till crazy hours about everything except politics. Some of her best friends are Zionists.

Is Ami out the army yet? The last time you wrote, he was "somewhere in the Sinai". I can't imagine that child a soldier. I hope he starts painting again, soon.

I'll send postcards from everywhere so's you can join me on my travels, vicariously, at least.

Love, Sara

WASHINGTON, 13 September 1973
Dear Pat,

Thanks again for your hospitality. London was marvellous, cool, civilised, as always. I'm still hoarse from all that talk. Yet so much was left unsaid. Should one say everything to friends?

New York was alive, vibrant, scary. I'm used to suppressed violence; here it's open, raw, physical. My neck hairs stood on end when we drove through Harlem. I've never felt that in Soweto. But for someone on leave from authoritarianism, it's a delight to see errant leaders hauled over the coals on TV.

Washington is, well, monumental. Those marble pillars will make splendid ruins one day.

Love, Sara

MONTEREY, 23 September 1973
Dear Dvora,

By now you've received my postcards from Chicago, San Francisco, Yosemite. I hate being a tourist, skimming surfaces. America is evading me. Cannery Row, like other places I've known from literature, was a disaster. Tourists, incense-scented shoppes, and not a malodorous cannery in sight.

My one-ness turns to lone-ness and I'm getting homesick. For where? Israel? England? South Africa? I feel fragmented. When I write to you I say, give back conquered territory, peace at any price. Who am I to speak? My children are in South Africa, not in border outposts. And when I write to Pat, I say, Israel has to survive, to have defensible borders.

I'll write again from Mexico.

Love, Sara

MEXICO CITY, 24 September 1973
Dear Pat,

Mexico's exciting. Modern industrial in some cities, half-pagan in the country-side. In spite of (because of?) four centuries of Catholicism, peasants still make offerings to the old gods, often with devastating effect. The combined might of the rain gods, Tlaloc, Chac and Cocijo, produced destructive floods last month, and the dead from the recent earthquake are still being counted. Nature's violent here, a tomb, not a womb. Small wonder the Aztecs bought off Huitzilopochtil with human hearts each day; they had to ensure the daily rebirth of the sun. I'd have hated to be an Aztec mother.

Love, Sara

MEXICO CITY, 26 September 1973
Dear Dvora,

The Pyramids at Teotihuacan are magnificent, mysterious. It's as well I'm seeing pyramids somewhere. I'll never get to Egypt.

The picture on this postcard is of the monument to Cuauhtemoc, the last Aztec Emperor. First they annihilate cultures, then they put up memorials.

Tonight's Rosh Hashana. Reckon if I can go to cathedrals, mission churches, mosques and Aztec temples, I can go to the synagogue, without abandoning unbelief.

Love, Sara

YUCATAN, 30 September 1973

Dear Pat,

In Mexico I'm an anthropology student, not a mere tourist, gods forbid. That macabre picture postcard I sent you from Chichen Itza, was of a Tzompantli, a Toltec skull rack. First the sacrificial victims lost their hearts, alive and beating, to the gods, then they had their heads stacked on this grim structure, with its bas-reliefs of death's head. My Mayan guide assured me that the Maya had been peace-loving, civilised people until the conquering Toltecs introduced human sacrifice. He forgot to add that in pre-Toltec times, virtuous virgins were ceremonially drowned in cenotes to propitiate the rain god Chac.

It's clear, however, why the Maya had a rain god, not a sun god. It's 102 in the shade at the moment.

Love, Sara

OAXACA, 5 October 1973

Dear Dvora,

It's marvellous to escape from one's own troubled culture for a while, but the perspective's been disheartening. There's this recurring theme of fear, ignorance, power abuse, sacrifice, bloodshed. And to what end? The gods are insatiable.

The picture on this postcard is of the ball court at Monte Alban. This ritual ball game was played all over pre-Columbian Mexico. The captain of the winning team was sacrificed to the gods. Some incentive. My fascination with these cultures is wearing thin; they're all pervaded with the smell of blood.

Tomorrow's Yom Kippur and I return to Mexico

City. I fast on Yom Kippur. Superstition? Propitiation? Identification? Who knows?

Love, Sara

MEXICO CITY, 7 October 1973
My dear Dvora,

I spent Yom Kippur at the Museum of Anthropology and didn't know war had broken out till evening. The first reports are dreadful, and my anxiety about all of you is unbearable. I watch TV, and wonder if your Ami is in one of those tanks rolling over the desert. I want to pack up and go home, and this time I know where home is.

Very little news comes through, and that which does, is conflicting. I tried to phone you but the lines are clogged. Please write. Just a few words. I'll be back in Johannesburg in three days.

Love, Sara

JOHANNESBURG, 10 October 1973
My dearest Dvora,

Please write, just a few words. I haven't been able to get through by phone.

Love, Sara

JOHANNESBURG, 21 October 1973
My dearest Dvora,

It was wonderful to hear your voice last night. Telephone conversations are almost as frustrating as letters, except that one receives an immediate reply. I'm so relieved everyone's well and that Ami is recovering from his injuries. You sounded so weary, so stoic. I'd have been a raving lunatic by now.

I wish the war was over, and that a permanent peace was made. The bloodshed, the dreadful bloodshed.

I've not written to Pat since the war. I can't bear to know what she's thinking. Our friendship would founder on words like "neo-imperialism" and "expansionism".

Love, Sara

JOHANNESBURG, 23 October 1973
Dear Pat,

Thanks for your letter. You ask about Dvora. I phoned her two days ago. She and her husband are well. Her daughter and her family got away from their kibbutz minutes before it was overrun by peace-loving Syrians. Her younger son, Ami, was wounded by grenade splinters in his left arm and leg. He's recovering and will soon be rejoining what's left of his unit.

Other news. Two of the youngsters from the kibbutz I lived on have been killed. One was the nineteen-year-old son of old friends. I didn't know the other boy. His parents joined the kibbutz after I left. They could've been my sons.

You ask why I haven't written. I'm afraid your views are the same as those of your fellow exiles, and I can't bear to hear them at the moment. Yet I need to know what you're thinking. We've skirted the issue for too many years. If you don't reply, I'll understand.

Yours, Sara

JOHANNESBURG, 26 October 1973
My dearest Dvora,

It's hard to write these days. What can I tell you? Our local Zionists have organised a Sacrifice Sale to raise money for Israel. What the hell's a sacrifice sale, I asked the collector. You give us something you don't want, and we sell it to someone who does. Now that's a sensible sacrifice. You don't lose your heart and head that way. I wanted to show him a drawing of an Aztec sacrifice.

I've written to Pat, asking her to tell me her views. I fear I'm losing a friend. Another contribution to the sacrifice sale, but one I'm reluctant to part with. Write soon.

Love, Sara

JOHANNESBURG, 28 October 1973

My dearest Dvora,

My psyche's slowly catching up with events; I've been having dreadful dreams. Last night I dreamed I was standing in a large, barren field, at the centre of which stood a Tzompantli, like the one I saw at Chichen Itza. The heads of beautiful young men were stacked on it. The chaverim from the kibbutz came across the field towards me and said, "Where have you been all these years. Look at our sacrifices." I turned away and wept.

"I'll come back," I said, "but spare my sons."

"Why are your sons more valuable than ours?" They pointed to the Tzompantli.

I woke, went downstairs, prepared breakfast for David and Gideon, drove them to school, then returned home. I wept till I was weary.

Once I questioned whether one should say everything to friends. Pat, I'm sure, won't reply to my letter. I hope you will, after I've said what's pressing on my heart. If I don't say it, it will lie like a shadow between us, forever.

I'm glad I left the kibbutz. I'm glad I don't live in Israel. I'm grateful my sons' heads don't lie on the skull rack, though I'm devastated about those that do.

Yours, with love and despair, Sara

JOHANNESBURG, 14 November 1984
Dear Pat,

I thought of you the other day when I sifting through old letters. They all belong to another life, another time. Only the Tzompantli, the Toltec skull rack, seemed real, and the daily sacrifice of human hearts to the gods. In retrospect, our ideological squabbles seem tame compared with those primal fears.

Thank you for your touching letter. I think and talk in cliches these days; it distances the pain. Hence, "life goes on". The official communique said that David's jeep had been blown up by a land mine during the retreat from Angola. Gideon stayed for a few weeks after the funeral, then returned to his ashram. In our day we sought salvation on the kibbutz.

Our plans for the future are vague. We'll probably remain on in South Africa; there's little point in leaving. Look after yourself. Life is precious.

Love, Sara

The Matriarch

The grandmother sits at the head of the table surrounded by her daughters, their spouses and her grandchildren. She listens, with a quizzical smile, to their laughter and lively arguments. "… can't be a traditional Jew without believing in God … a secular Jew, you mean … that's an oxymoron … grandma is …" Her silver-grey hair is drawn back in a bun, the severity of the style softened only by wisps of curly hair that escape over her forehead and ears. Her high cheek bones, short nose and black eyes, of Slavic or Tartar origin, remind Rachel of the men and women she had seen in the streets of St Petersburg the previous summer. They might have been her sisters, brothers, cousins. But they weren't. Her grandmother is the sole survivor of her family who had been massacred by the Nazis in 1941.

Rachel, at 24, is the oldest of her grandchildren. She had come to the apartment earlier that evening, without David, to help with the dinner. He's decided to take up the scholarship to Princeton, she told her grandmother. Will you join him? I wasn't invited, Rachel replied.

At the other end of table Rachel's father chants the blessing over the bread and wine. In one hand he holds the prayer book, in the other the silver wine goblet which reflects the dancing flames of the sabbath candles. Since the death of her grandfather, eight years ago, her father and her uncle take turns to make kiddush.

"You say you don't believe in God," Rachel's younger sister challenges her grandmother, "yet you light candles on Friday evening, go to synagogue on the Day of Atonement, and keep a kosher kitchen."

"I light candles because it reminds me of my parents' home, I go to shul on Yom Kippur to remember the dead, and I keep a kosher kitchen out of habit, I suppose. In the shtetl the rabbi's word was law. You either adhered to it or risked becoming a pariah."

"Did you adhere to it?"

The grandmother smiles. "If I hadn't, we wouldn't be sitting here today."

Rachel detects an ironic note in her voice.

Soon after dinner the grandchildren clear the table, pack the dishwasher, kiss their grandmother and go off to meet friends. Their parents set up the bridge table in the lounge. Rachel remains at the table with her grandmother.

"Doesn't it upset you when they rush off after dinner?"

"Not at all. We argue, laugh, catch up on the week's news, then it's time to go. No one has to glance at their watches or suppress yawns. Youth passes so quickly."

Rachel breaks off a piece of warm wax from the side of the candle and kneads it between her fingers.

"What's so marvellous about youth anyway? I want to be old and wise like you." Tears run down her cheeks.

"Tell me about David. I've never really spoken to him."

"Not much to tell. He's brilliant, ambitious, and wants to become a world-class scientist. And I'm just a run-of-the mill doctor who doesn't want to leave the country, friends or family."

"There's more, Rachel."

"Of course there's more. But I take after you. You also baulk at the truly personal. There are times when you're a complete enigma to me, grandma."

"How can you say that? I've told you so much about my life."

"But nothing of your feelings."

"What is there to tell? I left the shtetl to study in a larger town where I met a charming older man, a widower. We married and emigrated to Australia. When war seemed imminent, we tried to get my family out of Europe, but it was too late ..."

"There's more."

"Well, life in the shtetl wasn't as idyllic as I always paint it. The weather, except for a brief summer, was cold and miserable. The roads were unpaved and muddy, and our houses were small, airless. Although our parents struggled to make a living, my siblings and I managed to get an education. Among other things, I learned Russian at school, English in classes at the Workers' Club, and I had a wonderful Hebrew teacher ..."

"Tell me about the teacher."

"A teacher's a teacher, some are good, some not so good. During World War I we were exiled deep into the heart of Russia because the Tsar thought we'd spy for the Germans. And occasionally when the peasants became frustrated with their poverty-stricken lives, they'd turn on their Jewish neighbours and shout, 'Kill the Christ killers!'"

"There are ten or twelve years missing from your story, grandma. I worked out you were about 28 or 29 when you married Grandpa. That was considered old in the shtetl. You were a beautiful young woman, and must've had suitors. What happened during those missing years? I want to know where you go when you look into the distance and smile your Mona Lisa smile."

The grandmother sighs. "Now, at the age of 80, she wants me to bare my shrivelled soul. Even your mother never pressed me for such details. There are things I can't talk about."

"Try. It might help your Rochala face her own problems."

"Rochala. We named you after my mother ..."

"Tell me a story, Bobbala."

"Well ... I'll try. Amol is geven, is how Yiddish stories begin. Once upon a time, there was a small town, a shtetl, through which a beautiful river flowed. On one side of the river there was a synagogue, a cheder, the ritual baths, a school, several rows of shops, and the public baths. The Rabbi, the doctor, the pharmacist, and some well-off shopkeepers lived there. On the other side of the river lived the less affluent working people. Among them was a tailor, his wife and their five children, three boys and two girls. The youngest child was a girl. She was a lively, inquisitive child who wanted to do everything her brothers did, unlike her older sister who was pretty and gentle, and was happiest helping her mother cook and bake. The younger daughter, let's call her Mierke, used to follow her brothers to cheder where they learned Hebrew and studied the bible in preparation for their bar mitzvahs. The cheder teacher, a bad-tempered man with a large family and a small income, was mercilessly teased by his pupils. Go home! he'd shout at Mierke, waving his stick at her. Cheder is not for girls! She finally persuaded a much-loved older brother to teach her the rudiments of Hebrew reading and writing. When he could teach her no more, he handed her over to his best friend, the Rabbi's son Yossala, a brilliant boy."

Rachel leans her elbows on the table, face cupped in hands. The grandmother sips her lemon tea.

"Aren't you bored with these bobbemeises, these grandmother's tales? Sitting there, with your face in your hands, I'm reminded of you as a child, the kind Mierke might have been, taking in every word, wanting to know everything. Have you ever read Isaac Babel's story about a young boy and his grandmother? You must know everything, she used to tell him between his Hebrew and violin lessons. And all he wanted to do was to escape from the heated room, with its overwhelming smell of food, into the fresh air."

"Forget Babel. Go on with your story, grandma."

"Mierke and Yossala became close friends. He was like a fourth brother to her. But as they grew older, their friendship blossomed, as they say. Mierke's preparing her Hebrew lessons, her brothers would tease Yossala when he came to the house; she wants to impress her Hebrew teacher. He'd blush to the roots of his beautiful black hair and insist he'd come to visit them, not Mierke. He was a good teacher and she was a willing, if questioning, pupil. The Bible's full of smiting and slaying, slaughter and destruction, discomfiting and vengeance, she complained. And fear and awe of God. Where's the love? The world is beautiful. I want a joyous God. Wait till we get to the Psalms, he said. And don't blaspheme. He placed a finger gently over her lips. For a long time they sat looking at one another, knowing that their childhood friendship had passed into another phase."

"Is that all Mierke and Yossala ever did? Sat and read the Bible?"

"Of course not. In winter they skated on the frozen river, or sat with friends in the parlour, singing Yiddish songs, reading poetry, talking. And in summer they strolled through the woods, collecting wild strawberries. They lived in interesting times. A new era had begun after World War I. They were poor, but young and hopeful. Yossala was drawn to the ideas of the Enlightenment, but loved God more. The Hebrew lessons continued. Just listen to this, he'd exclaim as they worked their way through the Psalms:

'O Lord my God, thou art very great;
Thou art clothed with honour and majesty.
Who coverest thyself with light as with a garment;
Who stretchest out the heavens like a curtain;
Who layeth the beams of his chambers in the waters;
Who maketh the clouds his chariot;
Who walketh upon the wings of the wind ...'"

"How interesting, grandma, that you know exactly what Yossala read to Mierke."

"It is the privilege of the storyteller to know everything. And what she doesn't know, she invents. Which brings me to the time they read the *Song of Songs* for the first time ... But don't let me get distracted by the poetry which is even now running through my head. By this time, Yossala's father, the Rabbi, was getting worried. He had taught his son everything he knew and it was time for him to study at a Yeshiva, to become a rabbi. Yossala said he wasn't going anywhere and the Rabbi knew why. He did not want his son to marry into the family of an impecunious tailor; with his talent, he could marry into any of the famous rabbinic dynasties in the country. Yossala and Mierke met in the woods, put their arms around one another and wept. I'll never leave you, he vowed, not even for two years. I can't live without you ..."

"Brilliant though he was," Rachel murmurs, "Yossala couldn't live without Mierke."

"Nor I without you, Mierke told him. She had matured into a beautiful young woman, and a sensible one. Yossala, you must go to the Yeshiva. If you don't become a rabbi, you will break your father's heart, and he will always blame me for it. I will wait for you, forever if necessary."

The grandmother laughs, a little bitterly. "Only youth can make such terrible pledges: forever. What did they think they were? Immortal? Yossala came to a compromise with his father: he would go to the Yeshiva for two years but when he returned, he would marry Mierke. His father agreed. In two years, he told his wife, many things can happen. Imagine the parting, Rochala. She was seventeen, he twenty ..."

"I can imagine the parting."

"They wrote to one another all the time," says the grandmother, "quoting long passages from the *Song of Songs*. He wrote:

'Thou are beautiful, O my love, as Tirzah,
Comely as Jerusalem,
Terrible as an army with banners.
Turn away thine eyes from me,
For they have overcome me.
Thy hair is as a flock of goats,
That lie along the side of Gilead ...'

And she wrote back:
'Awake, O north wind; and come, thou South;
Blow upon my garden, that the spices thereof may flow out.
Let my beloved come into his garden,
And eat his precious fruits ...'

"Innocents. They scarcely understood what they were writing. They survived the separation, Yossala held his father to his word, and they were married. His parents, however, made plain their dissatisfaction with the match; this was not what they had planned for their son. But Yossala and Mierke were so absorbed in their love for one another, that they ignored the barbs and the disapproval. They lived happily for many years. She was content to be the young Rabbi's wife and filled her days with good works, tending to the sick and the poor. She kept a kosher home, washed and ironed, cooked and baked and mended clothes, for they had little money. But they had a secret sorrow: they did not have children."

"Did she and Yossala speak about it?"

"Rarely. He didn't want to shame her. We love one another, was all he said. Yossala, at this time, was having many arguments with his father. Rabbinical matters, he'd answer when Mierke asked what it was about; a difference in interpretation. When their tenth wedding anniversary approached, his father invited them for a meal at his home. After dinner, as he often did, he read a psalm. When he reached a certain passage, he looked across at Yossala. '... Happy shalt thou be, and it shall be well with thee. Thy wife shall be as a fruitful vine by the sides of thine house; Thy children like olive plants around thy table ...' Mierke lowered her head. Yossala appeared not to hear.

"Though they loved one another deeply, they gradually grew apart. She could not follow him into the world from which she, a woman, was excluded. He spent much of his day studying and writing learned treatises. Students and rabbis from all over the country came to consult with him, and as his father grew older, Yossala took over many of his rabbinic duties. And one day Mierke recognised her life in the Book of Proverbs:

'A virtuous woman, who can find?
For her price is far above rubies.
The heart of her husband trusteth in her,
And he shall have no lack of gain ...
All the days of her life
She seeketh wool and flax,
And worketh willingly with her hands ...
Her husband is known in the gates,
When he sitteth among the elders of the land
She maketh linen garments ...'

"From being spirited and joyful, from having an

enquiring mind and an independent spirit, Mierke had become a failed rebbetzin, one who could not bear children to sit like olive plants around their father's table. Everyone knows I am barren, she thought as she walked through the shtetl. They were pitying her, wondering when the young rabbi would cast her off.

"And one day, when Yossala was away in another town, her father-in-law entered the house, holy book in hand, like a prophet of doom. You must release him, he told Mierke, or you will ruin his life. He has the mind of a gaon, a genius, and could become the greatest rabbi in the land if he were not dragged down by you. After ten years of a childless marriage, it is his duty to divorce you, but he has a great fault, a misguided tenderness. If you truly love him, let him go. He tells me you are an intelligent woman, that you read much, write poetry. Leave him. Leave the shtetl. Go to a bigger town, study, forget him. Read Psalm 127 and know the truth of what I am telling you." He walked out of the house and she never saw him again."

"What did Mierke do?"

"First she read the psalm:

'... Lo, children are a heritage of the Lord,
And the fruit of the womb is his reward.
As arrows are in the hand of a mighty man,
So are children of youth.
Happy is the man that hath his quiver full of them;
They shall not be ashamed,
But they shall speak with the enemies in the gate.'

"I see you're wondering again at my remarkable memory, Rachel. I've read and reread these psalms over the years, and wondered, often, at the terrible price they exacted." Realising she has switched from the third to the first person, she smiles, but the smile does not reach her eyes. "The storyteller, as you must know by now, takes on the character of her creations. What did Mierke do, you ask. She lay on her bed and wept. That was where Yossala found her when he came home later that evening. They put their arms around each other and wept through the night. And when they could weep no more, she left the house, and went away to Riga, where her mother's sister lived. She was ill for a long time, and when she recovered, she studied to become a teacher, met a charming widower, an older man ..."

"And what happened to Yossala?"

"A year after Mierke left the shtetl, he married into one of the great rabbinic dynasties in the country. He fulfilled the great promise of his youth, and became a famous rabbi."

"And did he have children like olive plants around his table?"

"Alas no. Which was just as well, I suppose. They were married for about eight years when the war broke out, and in 1941, Yossala, his wife, and everyone else were massacred by the Nazis."

Give a Stone for Bread

Bessie Kekane lives in the north-eastern Transvaal in a village named after her grandfather. She is an old woman now. She was born and reared in that village, spent the middle years of her life as a domestic servant in the city, and has recently come home, not to die, she says, but to live among her kinsfolk who construct their homes from the stones that make their land unarable.

"Give a stone for bread," she weaves a mixed metaphor out of a common saw, giving it a biblical dimension, "and we shall build houses from it."

Her education at the local mission school has left her with a taste for scriptural cadences.

Since her return from the city she has had many visitors, mostly villagers whom she receives with the dignity expected of the granddaughter of a chief. There is also the occasional city caller who has discovered history. Bessie smiles, a little sadly, and says that until recently she had not even known when her people arrived in this corner of Africa, nor where they had come from. All she knew was that her grandfather had been born on the other side of the river, and that he had given his name both to the land and to the river that flows through it. By the time she was born, her tribe had been exiled to the arid, stony side of the river and its headwaters were dammed up to provide irrigation for what was to become one of the largest citrus estates in Africa, perhaps in the world. She points across the sluggish river towards the plantations that stretch across the Springbok Flats as far as the eye can see and says, "That was the land of my Ancestors."

Bessie had always been short and plump and even in her youth her legs had been slightly bowed. Today she is shorter and heavier, and her legs, half-crippled with arthritis, are so buckled, that she walks with the rocking motion of a person on a storm-tossed ship. She has a pretty face: a high brown forehead, part of which is covered by the scarf she wears over her wiry grey hair, yellow-brown tiger's eyes under arched, almost hairless brows, and a full-lipped mouth, bracketed between two genial lines that run from slightly flared nostrils to her chin.

"Mother Africa is kind to her children," she says of her otherwise unlined face.

When she is asked why she never married or had children, she smiles, the yellow lights in her eyes glow with humour and warmth, and, inverting the Mother Africa image, she says, "I got plenty children. All Africa is my children."

"You're telling me," Emma, her employer of forty years, used to add, "and I have to feed them all."

Emma was a tall, thickset English woman who had come to South Africa in her mid-twenties — she was as old as the century — equipped only with a degree in Fine Arts and a passion for doing good. She became active in the trade union movement where she met Donny, a history graduate who worked on the mines as a clerk; times were hard and academic posts difficult to get. Emma had a booming voice and an upper-class accent. The first she used for addressing factory workers; the second for pulling rank on their bosses. She helped organise one of the first women's trade unions in the country before she reverted to her first love, art, but she never "sold out".

"In other words," Donny told the young woman who interviewed him some years after Emma's death, "she never made a living."

By the time Bessie came to work for them, Emma and Donny had already opened the small art gallery in the city where they exhibited work of black painters and sculptors long before black art became fashionable. Consequently, they had little money. Had it not been for the picture-framing workshop which Donny, who was very good with his hands, had set up in the shop next door, they would have had to close the gallery. The city's intelligentsia were extravagant in their praise for scenes of black township life and the rough-hewn sculpture of indigenous people and animals, but few of them bought anything but prints of Van Gogh's sunflowers, Monet's water lilies and Renoir's buxom beauties which Donny had providently acquired over Emma's cries of "philistine!" A sharp-tongued woman who was known as the Gorgon or the Dragan, epithets of which she was well aware and secretly relished,

Emma did not hesitate to excoriate the tastes of prospective buyers.

"Which did little," Donny told the young interviewer whose name was Corinne and who was doing a Ph.D on the role of women in the South African trade union movement, "to contribute towards the rent. Top you up?" Corinne shook her head and took a sip of her lime juice. Donny poured himself another whisky. Why, he wondered, were all latter-day suffragettes or libbers or whatever they called themselves, flat-chested? Emma had been generously endowed.

Bessie and Emma had clashed at first sight.

"We can't pay you much but you eat what we eat and you have quite a nice room upstairs. You'll have to use our bath, preferably during the day when we're at work, because there are only cold showers in the servants' quarters. And there's no madam-master talk here. I'm Emma, he's Donny and you're Bessie. Right?"

"Right, Madam."

"Emma! Emma! Not Madam! I can't bear servility."

Bessie drew herself up to her full four-foot-eight inches and looked into Emma's fierce blue eyes, embedded between crepey lids and deeply-scored crows' feet. Her grey hair spiked out like an icy halo around her head, and she seemed to breathe fire through her long, high-bridged nose.

"My grandfather," Bessie said, taking a deep breath, "he was Chief of the tribe. My father, he was a younger son. He sent me to the school and I can read and write. I also learned church manners. You must show respect to old people. So I call you madam."

"Old people! How old are you?"

"Twenty-six."

"Never mind. Call me Emma. We're at the gallery all day and when we come home, we expect to find the apartment clean and dinner prepared. There isn't much washing and ironing to be done, so you can have most of the afternoons to yourself. We do expect you to stay in when we have guests, however."

Emma and Donny often had guests.

"You'll curdle the milk," Emma would say as Bessie, with queenly gestures, removed the dinner debris from the table. "I told you to rest up in the afternoons when we were having people to dinner. The darker our guests," she muttered to Donny, loudly enough for Bessie to hear, "the more acerbic her manner."

"This is my job, what can I do? It is better if you can be an artist," Bessie responded wearily, "but I am only a servant."

"Don't pull your guilt bit on me," Emma said sharply. "You've got damn-all to do all day."

"If Madam isn't satisfied ..."

"Emma! Not Madam!

"You can talk very nice," Bessie continued relentlessly, certain she would not be fired for lack of servility, "'Emma, not Madam'. And you never say kaffir or native, always African this and African that. But really, I am a slave for you."

"Of all the ungrateful ...! Who helps you educate that tribe of nieces and nephews who are always hanging around? Who got your brother Elijah a pass and a job? Who sends food parcels to your mother in that godforsaken hole your grandfather was chief of? That's your trouble; you're full of fantasies about your tribal past. Your grandfather was probably nothing more than a successful cattle rustler ..."

At this point Bessie clutched her head and wailed with impotence. And Emma, knowing she had gone too far, went further.

"And once we're on that subject, I might tell you I resent your rustling my beef to feed your hangers-on."

It usually took a few days before Donny could persuade Emma to apologise, and Bessie to withdraw her resignation.

"She's a gem," he remonstrated with Emma. "Honest, loyal, a good cook. When any of our friends finds a passable cook, she falls pregnant and leaves."

"No one falls pregnant in this apartment," Emma snapped. "You should try giving her an instruction once in a while, she takes any crap from you. Royal blood indeed. She's always going on about chief this and chief the other. The ignorant woman doesn't realise that the only way the Africans will liberate themselves will be to sink their tribal differences and form one nation."

The substance of this argument remained constant, only "African", over the years, gave way to "Black".

"If you've ever wondered what it would be like to see Boadicea and Mantitisi lock horns, you'd have appreciated the fights between Emma and Bessie," Donny said to Corinne. She shook her straight blond off her forehead, narrowed her slanting green eyes, then asked whether Emma had been active in the 1922 Revolt. Donny smiled; Corinne had not done her homework. "Emma only arrived in Africa in 1925," he said.

"Bessie," he continued as Corinne suppressed a yawn and began to doodle in her notebook, "finally resorted to guerilla tactics. She was a regular mangonel, though stones were no match for Emma's sophisticated armoury of verbal barbs. Being a student of history you'll know, of course, what a mangonel is," he added as Corinne glanced up, her ballpoint pen suspended in the air.

Bessie's guerilla tactics included calling Emma "Madam" in the presence of her liberal friends; singing hymns as she stood over the kitchen sink — Emma was an unrelenting atheist — and dropping plates and glasses with daunting regularity. When she wanted to express extreme displeasure, she stopped bathing.

"You tell her," Emma said to Donny.

"Doesn't bother me. I don't mind the smell of honest human sweat. Rather like boiled onions, wouldn't you say?"

Emma described it in a series of succinct scatological phrases.

Finally, in a cold rage, aware that Bessie had once again manoeuvred her into a calculated stalemate, she told her to bath. Bessie assented at once, with a serene smile. She was Emma's scourge; she never let her forget she was a white madam.

"Why didn't they part?" Donny echoed Corinne's impatient question. "Because they needed one another, that's why. And why did I leave the dirty work, as you so delicately put it, to Emma? Because I had no desire to get crushed between these women of granite. They thrived on their battles. The only time their relationship was really threatened was when these childless Amazons fought for the soul of Shikwane, or Samuel as he was known as a child."

Shikwane was the son of Bessie's brother Elijah who was ten years younger than her and who lived in the city. He had come to visit Bessie one Saturday afternoon with his two-year-old child when Emma walked into the kitchen. Bessie's parlour, she called it.

"He was named after our grandfather, Shikwane, but he was baptised Samuel," Elijah told Emma. She took a sweet out of a glass jar and knelt down to give it to the little boy.

"Beautiful child," Emma murmured when he smiled shyly, revealing dimples in his cheeks.

Bessie issued a stern instruction in Ndebele, and Samuel clapped his hands before he took the sweet.

"This hand clapping is ..." Emma began, then remembered that one did not speak of servility to Bessie.

"Doggie, doggie," Samuel said, patting Emma's grey hair gently with his free hand.

"Everything with soft hair he calls doggie," Elijah smiled apologetically. "He loves dogs."

"I've been called worse things in my life," Emma said, lifting the child. He put his soft arms around her neck, laid his head against hers and said, "Doggie, doggie."

"We try to speak English to him," Elijah said, "so that it will be easier for him to live in the city."

"Ai." Bessie clucked disapprovingly. "He must know his own language."

"It's good you're teaching him English," Emma said as she put him down. "He'll know his own language anyway. Bring him here again, soon, and start looking around for a good school. I'll help you pay for his education."

"She was an impossible woman," Bessie says of Emma, "but she had a kind heart. She helped me with the children of my family, even when she did not have much money. She did not know how to speak with children and they were a little bit frightened of her. But not Shikwane. He was not frightened of anyone, of anything. When she picked him up that time I saw she had tears. I think it was the first time she had a child in her arms. I'm not sure. She loved Shikwane, too much." And Bessie sighs deeply; the wound is still fresh.

"She was besotted with the child," Donny told Corinne. "Me? Sure I loved him. I had wanted to adopt a child when we were younger, but Em always refused; it would interfere with her work, she claimed. She'd always preferred black babies; white ones were doughy, she said. When he was older, Samuel, or Shikwane as he later called himself, spent every weekend with us. First he slept in Bessie's room at the top of the building, then Emma bought a sofa-bed for the study."

"Work, not wek; church, not chech," Emma said to Shikwane. "Look at my mouth, child. Chu-rr-ch, roll your tongue, that's right, that's right! You deserve another kiss and hug for that. And your mother, your real mother, is a she, not a he; your father's hat is his hat, not her hat ..."

"We are two sisters and three brothers in my family," Bessie says, "and only Elijah lives in the city, even now." She shakes her head. "I am the oldest, he is the youngest. The others" — she draws a circle in the air — "live all around me in the village. Only the men, when they were young, went to the city to look for work." She says 'wek'. "The women all worked on the orange estate, digging, planting, picking. Except me. I wanted to be a teacher so I went to the city to earn money for study. I could not afford to study but the children of my brothers and sisters, they studied. One is a teacher, another a bookkeeper, a third is a nurse ..."

She lists the occupations of her fourteen nieces and nephews. "That house" — she points out of the window to a hovel made of the white stones which the earth throws up here with wanton prodigality — "was my mother's. We keep it for when the children visit. This house I have built." She smiles. "I say I have built, like the white people say, we mowed the lawn, we cleaned the house, we did the washing. Maybe I was too long in the city."

"Yes," Bessie goes on, "the children visit here often, all of them. Some, they are working in the towns not far from here, others are in the village — the teacher, the nurse, the post office clerk, the bookkeeper. Only Shikwane was in the city. And the Madam was like a granny for him. When Elijah first brought him to the flat, she was nearly sixty years old. In the beginning he liked too much to come to the flat. Every week, every week he comes, and the Madam is waiting, waiting. Bessie cook this, Bessie cook that. Samuel likes it, she tells me. Look what we cooked for you, she says when he comes." Bessie smiles.

"Emma displayed more tact during that period than ever in her life," Donny told Corinne. "How, after all, could an ageing white woman entertain a black child in a segregrated city? She couldn't take him to the movies, he wasn't allowed to play on the swings in the park, she couldn't even give him lunch at a steakhouse. Nor could she walk him around the block without causing a mild sensation: see that crazy white bitch walking the little kaffir boy? I'm not exaggerating, Corinne; that's how it was in the sixties. And the seventies, for that matter. But Emma found ways to amuse him."

She read to him, showed him books with paintings,

gave him a box of crayons, then water colours, then oil paints. "He's got an eye," she said, "a feel for form and colour. Samuel, my child, one day we'll mount a one-man show for you."

She taught him to handle table cutlery, to keep his elbows off the table, to spread his serviette over his knees when he ate. Bessie was apprehensive. He will not want to live with his brothers, she thought. To counteract Emma's influence, she took him to the village whenever she could. At first he was bored. Later he made friends with boys his age. They set traps for birds, climbed the aloe-covered hills, skimmed stones across the river, and raided the orange groves on the outskirts of the village.

"That's stealing," Bessie admonished him. "You can buy a whole bag of oranges for thirty cents, you don't have to steal. If Madam knew about it, she'd say you take after your great-grandfather. She calls him a cattle rustler."

"We only take one or two oranges," Samuel said, his eyes sparkling with mischief. "We do it to keep the watchman awake, otherwise he sleeps all day. He's too fat to catch us, anyway. Besides," he teased Bessie, "you always say the land belongs to us."

"Not the oranges. You'll disgrace us all one day, the great-grandson of a chief."

"Tell me about him."

"I don't know much," Bessie said, "but there are old people in the village who still remember."

By now he was speaking Ndebele fluently. He set about seeking out the old people.

"They tell me many stories," he said to Emma when he returned from the village.

"What kind of stories?"

He told her about Musi, the great chief who came from far away Zululand to the Transvaal about three hundred years ago. He had a son called Tshwane, who had six wives, each of whom had a son. These sons mapped out their own territories and started their own tribe. One of them was called Moletlane, and he was the ancestor of the Kekana tribe.

"That's my tribe," he said. "My great-grandfather, Shikwane, is his descendant. He was also called Mabediela which means the one who makes peace, and the name of our place, Zebediela, comes from that. I want to be called Shikwane, not Samuel from now on," he concluded breathlessly.

Bessie listened attentively; she had heard about Musi but did not know about his six sons and the tribes they established. The old people did not talk much about the past; they were too weighed down by the present.

"More chiefs," Emma said in disdain, but her heart grew cold; she was losing out to Bessie and the tribalists. "My dear boy, if you're really interested in history, we can go to the Africana Library where we'll find accounts by anthropologists who have studied the tribes of Africa. The stories you hear from the old people are myths, made up to explain something they don't understand. Like the Hebrews with their twelve tribes. All cultures have myths and they're very entertaining, but one shouldn't make the mistake of believing them."

"That was a mistake," Donny said to Corinne, "a serious lapse in her hard-won tact. Emma took Shikwane to the Africana Library. 'I'm sorry ma'am,' the librarian said, shame-faced, 'this library is for whites only. They do have library services in the black townships.' Emma's response registered 7.5 on the Richter scale. That was about three years before the 1976 uprising in Soweto. Samuel was only twelve then. Emma wasn't sure how this incident affected him, but she did say he was very quiet on the way home."

"Shikwane understood too much, even when he was small," Bessie says. "That time when Madam took him to the library, he was very much upset. I will never go there again, he told me, but he did not say what happened."

"Yes, my dear, I realise that your interest is in Emma and the early trade union movement, but you can't really understand Emma without seeing her in relation to Bessie and her family. What you should try to understand is that there was a living, feeling, suffering woman behind the public one." Donny refilled his glass. He did not offer to top up Corinne's lime juice this time. "No, Emma was never a member of the Communist Party. Nor, for that matter, was she a nudist, a vegetarian or a Rosicrucian."

When Samuel became Shikwane, he began withdrawing from Emma. He came to the apartment less frequently, rarely staying the weekend, and spent more and more time in the township with his friends. When he did visit, much of his time was spent in Bessie's parlour. Emma's heart ached when she listened to the easy talk between them, the laughter. But when she heard them sing hymns, she decided to fight back. It was one thing to make a tribalist out of Samuel; it was quite another to convert him into a hymn-singing handclapper. If she could not compete with his Ancestors, she would co-opt them, work with them against the insidious Believers.

"He was full of mischief," Bessie recalls with a smile. "He loved to laugh. He knows I like to sing the Church hymns, so when he comes to visit me, he teaches me new words for old hymns. When you go to church, he says to me, you must make your face long, holy, and you must sing the words of Amaboer Lamaleka ... Yes, he was nearly fifteen when the trouble started in Soweto, but he was already singing those songs about our worries and the police. The children learn early in the townships."

"Have you heard more stories from the old people?" Emma asked when Shikwane came to visit. He smiled and shook her hand; he no longer greeted her with a kiss. She longed to reach out, to touch him, but she held back. He was growing so tall, so straight, she thought with pride.

"Oh yes. When I was home for Easter."

"You should write them down." She winced at the word home. "One day you'll go to university, study history and disentangle myth from reality. Enough strangers have told your story."

"I would like that," he said shyly, "but my English writing is not so good. Our English teacher at school does not teach us so good."

"So well," Emma corrected. You spend too much time in the village and in the township, she wanted to add. "That's not so important at this stage," she said instead. "Just write them down and show them to me. I'm very interested. It's a pity you don't find time to paint any more," she added, but changed the subject when he lowered his head and frowned.

The following week he brought Emma an exercise book in which he had written three stories in his rounded, childish script. She flicked through it, stopping to read a story he called Blind Bulongo.

"There is Kekane also in another place, not Zebediela, which is called Hammanskraal," she read with a sinking heart. "The main chief was Bulongo. When this chief was old and blind he wanted to give the medicine and other things of his chief rule to his eldest son Manala. Go hunt a mbudumo, he says to him, which is a zebra. The mother of Ndzundza did hear this. She was Bulongo's small wife, not the chief one. She did tell Ndzundza to go kill a goat and she cooked it. Ndzundza did pretend to be Manala and he took the food to him and because Bulongo was blind, he did think it was his son Manala and did give him the rhino horn and the medicine horn which will make him chief. When Manala came home he was very cross because now his younger brother was the chief. And when his father did die, he took his people and they did chase away Ndzundza and his people and Manala became chief."

"And she did tell, and he did think, and his father did die…" Emma exploded. "What sort of English is that? As for the story itself, it comes straight out of the Old Testament, Jacob and Esau. These Christianised black people are distorting their own history, superimposing one kind of myth on another."

"It was Emma's strength and weakness," Donny told Corinne, draining his glass, "that she couldn't sell out, not even for the love of Samuel-Shikwane. She was a compulsive truth teller. We rarely saw him after that, though Emma continued to pay his school fees. Bessie told me later that he used to visit her during the week when we were at work. Then, of course, there was the uprising ... Afterwards Emma gathered together all Shikwane's painting and drawings and burned them. "The waste, the sheer and utter waste of it all," she said. "But there's no point in this sentimental hoarding." I knew, however, that the most important part of her life had gone up in those flames. 'You can do the same for me one day,' she said briskly. And I did. I did."

Donny laughed as he limped across the room to the little table on which a small tape recorder stood. Humming to himself he took a cassette from a large stack and inserted it into the machine.

"Chopin's Largo in E Flat major," he said. Corinne stood up. "Don't go yet, my dear. This is one of the most beautiful pieces of music I know. Emma's passion was art, mine is music. I had to sell my hi-fi equipment and all our paintings because I can't manage on my pension. I gave all our furniture to Bessie and moved into the Home. But I can't do without music. So I record concerts from the radio onto these old tapes ... That's better, sit a while, everything's relevant. Friends keep me in whisky. The opiate of the asses."

"And what happened to all those people I cooked for every night, every night?" Bessie shrugs and turns her pale work-worn palms upwards. "When things got bad, the visitors did not come any more. The black artists took their things to other galleries. The rent was too much and Donny did close the shop and the gallery. And afterwards, after the Soweto troubles, Emma was very sick. She did not know anybody. The doctor said it was a stroke and she must go to hospital. But me and Donny did not let her go. He went to the study to sleep on Shikwane's sofa and I was with Emma, every day, every night. She did not know me, only my hands.

I washed her, gave her the food, cleaned her mess. When Donny comes in she looks at him and looks at him and says, 'Where's the young man who used to live with me?' I never did see Donny cry so much, ever, not even when she died."

"Who finally won the battle for Shikwane's soul? Now that's a nice human question to ask," Donny smiled approvingly at Corinne. "The Angel of Death, of course. But briefly, before that, I'd say Emma had the edge over Bessie and the tribalists. She was sinking so fast, however, that she never knew it."

Bessie goes to the sideboard and takes out a dog-eared exercise book from a drawer.

"All his stories," she tells her visitor. She touches it tenderly with her fingertips. "But it was hard for him to make them."

"I don't know what to believe any more," Shikwane told Bessie after yet another weekend in the village. "I hear stories from this one and stories from that one. Shikwane was a great chief, they tell me. He helped his people very much. Good, I say. But if he helped them so much, why did they have to move off the land of their ancestors to this side where there is nothing but stones and dust? They do not know. When did they have to move? They cannot remember. If he was such a good chief, why are we slaves? Surely it is better to be dead than to be a slave, I say to them. The old people look at me and shake their heads. I am not a peace-maker like my great-grandfather."

Bessie frowned. "You must not speak like that to the old people."

"I must know, I need to understand. How can you understand what is happening now if you don't know what happened before? They tell me that Shikwane was called Mabediela because he was a peace-maker. I must find out. The libraries are open to the blacks now. I swore I would never there again, but I must. Perhaps I will find the answer in their books."

"I want to know the history of Zebediela," he said to the librarian. He could not remember if this was the same woman Emma had shouted at three years ago.

"Sit there." She pointed to a long wooden table. He felt stiff, uncomfortable, an intruder in the large room lined with glass-fronted bookcases. There was only one other person in the library, an elderly white man who was reading a large leather-bound book from which he made notes on a sheet of paper. Next time, Shikwane decided, I will bring my exercise book. The librarian riffled through some cards in a large wooden file, scribbled a few notes on a piece of paper, and took out two booklets from a cupboard. "I'll have to go down to the store for the other one," she said.

"In one book, Zebediela Estate, there is a picture of orange groves on the cover," Shikwane told Bessie, "It says that after World War I someone called Schlesinger planted the orange groves. He was the chief and he is buried on a hill overlooking Zebediela. Like our chiefs, in our land." Shikwane smiled bitterly. "He bought the land from Gilfillan, but I can't find who this Gilfillan bought or stole the land from."

When he visited Bessie the following week, Shikwane looked depressed. "It's getting more difficult," he said, opening his exercise book. "Listen to this: 'Towards the end of the 1800s the Amandebele tribe on the southern slopes of the Strydpoort Mountains in the North-Eastern corner of the Springbok

Flats was ruled by Shekoene Kekana, a shrewd and diplomatic chief whose tactful settlement of tribal affairs earned him the name of Mabediela — the one who pacified ..." This means they bought him. In another book, *The Native Tribes of the Transvaal*, I find this, 'Shikwane's tribe is the only one in the Transvaal suspected of having concealed rifles at the disarmament in 1903 ... Shikwane was sullen in demeanour ...' Much better. We made resistance. But which one is true?"

Bessie presses the exercise book against her heart. "In here, he wrote all these stories which I never before heard in my life. Even the old people don't know this. Then one day he comes to me and his face is grey. Always he goes to the cookie tin to see what I have baked. This time he sits down and doesn't speak. Then he opens this book." Bessie mimics his actions and begins to read very slowly from the exercise book ...

"In the Sekukuni War of 1852 waged by the South African Republic against the Pedi, Zebediela supplied a contingent of 400 auxiliaries in addition to furnishing supplies of corn and cattle to the Boers. In return, the Zebediela clan were exempted from taxation for a while and in 1885 a location was beaconed off by the Republic for them."

Bessie straightens out the dog-eared pages and says, "I can see Shikwane is in a dangerous mood. 'Maybe the Pedi people was our enemy in those days,' I told him. There was a lot of fighting between the different tribes. I'm sure my grandfather, the chief, did every-thing he could for his people. But I can see I am losing Shikwane; he doesn't listen to me any more. He is looking far away. 'Sold out,' he says, 'and so cheaply.'"

Bessie pages through the exercise book, reluctant to put it down.

"Shikwane did not go any more to the village, and he did not come any more to the flat. And soon afterwards there was the trouble in Soweto. I worried very much. From when he was a small child Shikwane was already singing those songs that used to be church hymns. Emma was also very much worried. Go to the township, Bessie, go find out what is happening there. So I go. I was there when they brought in his body. They shot him together with two of his friends. They were throwing stones at the Boere on the armoured cars, the hippos."

Bessie walks slowly to the sideboard, opens a drawer and puts the exercise book away.

"We build our houses from these stones," she says, staring out of the window. "But our young ones make tombstones from them."

"Well, if you really must go," Donny says, standing up as Corinne puts her pen and notebook into her bag. "I hope our little chat was useful. You know, of course, that Emma started writing her autobiography. Well, not exactly writing it; she talked it onto tapes. You didn't know? Well, imagine that. Shows how much interest everyone showed in her while she was alive. Yes indeed. All our spare money went on tapes. She sat for hours talking into the tape recorder, that very one standing on the little table. The only trouble was that after Shikwane's death in 1976, she suffered a stroke from which she never fully recovered. Some of her stuff made sense. The rest was rambling nonsense. The tapes? I've used most of them to record music from the radio. No point in sentimental hoarding, as Emma said when she burned Samuel/Shikwane's paintings. Besides, I promised Emma I would do for her what she had done for him. Mind the step, my dear, you nearly tripped. And if you really want to know how Emma ticked, go to the village and speak to Bessie. She understood her better than anyone else did."

House Arrest

1

A perfect setting for a house arrest. As she drives up the sand road towards the house, Nathalie wonders whether Miriam will see it her way. Immured by pine trees on three sides, blending in with the rocks and thorn trees that frame it, the house seems grafted into the hillside, a suburban prison, complete with wrought-iron window bars: three pairs of curved shapes, like birds in flight, impaled by vertical bars.

Following the aroma of freshly baked bread, Nathalie finds Miriam in the kitchen.

"I thought you were giving up domestic drudgery for the piano, Miriam."

"I will, as soon as school holidays are over." Miriam wipes a streak of flour across her cheek. "Weren't you seeing Fuchs this morning?"

"At twelve fifteen. By which time I have to provide him with an address for Judith."

"I thought that decision was made."

"I can't have her. My father will freak out. He'll have a heart attack."

"He threatened to have one when you divorced Robbie. That didn't prevent you from doing what you wanted."

"He didn't speak to me for a year."

"Three weeks."

"And he landed up in hospital."

"With piles."

Nathalie shrugs and looks out the window. Matthew, the gardener, is sweeping dead leaves towards a little fire under the pines, his metal rake rasping over the dry winter grass. The smell of burning leaves sifts through the dark pines, mingling with the scent of peach blossom and newly baked bread. "Voetsek!" Matthew shouts as Zorba and Boubalina, orphans of a stray bitch Miriam saved from the gas ovens, tear through neat piles of leaves: Ecru-oo-oo, ecru-oo-oo, a dove sings out the colour of the grass. It is a secluded place, a healing place. Judith could find peace here.

"She's counting on us."

"She's counting on you." Miriam is angry, defensive. "She's your friend. And Helen's. You worked with Judith on the Daily Mail for nine years. And Helen knows her from way back in Young Communist League days. You promised to take her in when she came out of jail. Besides, Bernard and I hardly know her."

"I have problems …"

"Who hasn't? Bernard's working on a new novel and there's a mass of banned literature in our house. They're bound to search. Imagine their faces when they come across the *Communist Manifesto*. Imagine Bernard in a dark, murky cell. He'll go mad, cooped up in a cell. The Ninety Day Act, detention without trial …"

"Hundred and Eighty Day Act," Nathalie corrects. "I don't know what you're going on about. Anyway, Bernard could do with an injection of real life experience. His characters are stereotypes. In his last book there was that Special Branch man in a trench coat. Tall, cropped blond hair, icy blue eyes. He's seen too many espionage films. He might even be grateful for the experience."

"I know Bernard. He won't be grateful. Besides, there are other difficulties. Mary's working here illegally. She's a prohibited migrant from Mozambique. They'll send her home, and her family depends on her wages. She's got three kids, an aged mother. Not to speak of my mother. You said you'd speak to Judith's parents. Surely they'd take her in after all she's been through."

"I phoned them last night. Mr Fletcher dredged up the headlines of yesteryear: Accused of plotting overthrow of the State; Wild interracial parties; Liaison with a married man. Old Fletcher was bitter. His grandparents, he informed me, had worked in the Ciskei as missionaries among the Natives. Generations of Fletchers had lived by the belief that all people, black and white, were equal in the eyes of the Lord. Only Judith had become depraved in her zeal to prove it. I tried to explain that times had changed, that Judith's concern with justice was as pure as their own — and not so damned patronising and paternalistic, I wanted to add. He didn't want to know. A sinful woman, he said before he banged down the phone on me, can hardly lead the Native out of Barbarism."

Miriam looks tearful.

"Ah well, I'll fix up the servant's room in my backyard, and when my father comes to visit, Judith can move in there. She's been in worse places."

She picks up her bag and walks to the door. "Sorry Miriam. Perhaps I press too hard. Why should you take Judith in? As you say, you hardly know her. We're her friends, and with friends like us she doesn't need enemies."

"You visited her in jail, sent her parcels, books ..."

"Big deal. We're losing our humanity in this hell-hole. The Government doesn't have to oppress or censor us. We do it all ourselves. Your burglar proofing says it all. We live in prisons of our own making."

"And I'm chief warder," Miriam says, walking with her to the car. "Listen, when Bernard comes back from University, I'll speak to him. He had a long talk with Judith at one of your parties. He says she's an intelligent woman."

"Praise indeed from Bernard. I must rush off. Can't keep the Captain waiting."

Nathalie drives through the slow-moving traffic, angry with herself, irritated with Miriam, anxious to get to her appointment in time. She hates this soulless city which grew out of the mining camp on its western outskirts. Her childhood memories are of a different city, with tree-lined, cobbled streets, old stone buildings, and wrought iron street lamps. Their high-ceilinged apartment had stood on such a street. Then came the whispered conversations, tears, feverish activity, the dismantlement of the apartment, together with their lives. Late one night she and her mother had boarded the ship and watched her father grow smaller and smaller as the ship drew away from the quay. I'll be on the next boat, he promised. Six years had passed before they met again.

As she crosses a south-flowing street, she catches a glimpse of the mine dumps. Once, every southerly wind had deposited dust over the mining town and its denizens. Reeds and grass were planted in the arid soil of the dumps, taming its spread, disguising its origin, but like the patches of yellow sand that show through the covering, the denizen is still discernible in the citizen. The dumps stretch along the gold reef like mangy watch-dogs, guarding the approaches to the city. To the south-west lie the black townships.

She drives in the middle lane, flanked by vehicles in the outer lanes which peel off into intersecting streets. She moves slowly, inexorably, towards the L-shaped building at the end of the street. No retreat, only the westward thrust into its maws ... Get a hold on yourself, Nathalie, and remain calm for the interview. She leans away from the hot car seat. The smell of leather, petrol and exhaust fumes set off a nervous ripple in her stomach. There is nothing sinister about the building. Blue steel panels separate windows from concrete walls; glassed-in passages look onto the street, light and transparent. No hint of dark dungeons or windowless interrogation rooms. Nor does the building block off the road. It stands on the curve of a street which veers sharply to the left, creating an illusion of a cul de sac. She looks at her watch: five minutes to twelve. Her appointment with Captain Fuchs is for twelve-fifteen.

The street curves to the left; she turns right, into the square of the L-shaped building. The size and function of police buildings have certainly changed over the years. She used to pay traffic fines at her local police station, a renovated suburban house whose internal walls had been knocked down to create the Charge Office, a large room with a heavy oak counter and dark green walls. A partition separated blacks from whites. The constable spoke indifferent English to the whites, abusive Afrikaans to the blacks. Ten rand cash, no cheques excepted ... Pas, Kaffir! ... If you dropped a few coins into the collection box for the Police Orphans' Fund, you might be called Madam. Behind the counter was a small desk stacked with papers, files and an old-fashioned telephone. The constable clumped across the wooden floor, withdrew a small cash box from a wall safe, wrote out a yellow receipt, in triplicate, and slid it across the counter for signature. Until Judith was arrested, payment of traffic fines had been Nathalie's sole reason for visiting police stations.

A yellow Volkswagen, driven by a young man in a T-shirt, jeans and dark glasses, screeches to a halt beside her. Two large Alsatian dogs stand on the back seat, their tongues hanging out, panting from the heat. Seconds later, a police van draws up behind the Volkswagen. A black policeman jumps out, swinging his baton. He opens the back of the van and about twenty handcuffed black men stumble out, helped along by the swinging baton. The dog handler stands by, his animals straining at their leashes, barking furiously.

Nathalie waits in the car until the prisoners disappear into the building. She counts the number of floors in the building. Nine. No, ten. She'd last seen Fuchs on the sixth floor of their old headquarters on the other side of town. He had been cool and remote, silently noting her request to send Judith, who was serving a three-year sentence at Barberton Prison, some additional books. Then he stood up, indicating the interview was over.

After the handcuffed prisoners are herded out of the vestibule, Nathalie goes inside. A plain-clothes guard is sitting behind the reception desk.

"I have an appointment with Captain Fuchs," she says in Afrikaans, giving her name.

He dials a number. "Mrs Cohn to see you ... okay." He turns to her. "Take the lift to the ninth floor," he tells her.

Three lifts stand waiting, their doors open. The buttons in the first lift are numbered one to eight. The second lift shows basement, ground floor and seven other floors. The third lift is identical. She steps back, puzzled.

"Excuse me," she says to the cleaner who is washing down the tiled floors with a large mop. "I'm supposed to go to the ninth floor, to see Captain Fuchs, but these lifts only go to the eighth floor."

"Yes, missus." He wipes up the last of the dirt and places the mop inside the bucket. "The missus can come with me."

He ambles off ahead of her. Only the click of her heels and the shuffle of the cleaner's worn boots echo down the long, empty corridor. No other sound emerges from behind the closed doors on either side of them. There is a strong smell of fresh paint and damp concrete as they turn down another passage. Perhaps the offices are still unoccupied; the building was completed only a short time ago. The silence unnerves her.

After what seems an interminable walk, they reach a

flight of stairs leading into the basement. It is filled with cars.

"Where are all the people?" she asks the cleaner.

"Wekking."

She longs to ask where they are working, but decides against it, following him to a single lift shaft which stands unobtrusively among the cars.

"Press maar die button," he says. He claps his hands together before accepting the money Nathalie puts into his damp, calloused palm. "Dankie, Missus," he says, and shuffles off.

She enters the lift. One button is marked "Up", another, "Down". The rest are blank. Like a dream sequence from a Bergmann film: the clock without numbers, a coffin slithering out of a black hearse. Blank lift buttons. She's been seeing too many movies. Helen should've come with her. She's known Judith even longer than Nathalie has. She's so keen to take up that scholarship to Cambridge, that she no longer takes risks. Nathalie presses the "Up" button apprehensively. The doors close quietly and it moves swiftly upwards, coming to a halt with a slight bump.

When the doors open, she finds herself facing into a small lobby where an elderly man in a brown suit sits behind a sleek desk, reading a newspaper. She steps back involuntarily, her hand reaching for the "Down" button. The man smiles benignly, looking at her over the top of his glasses. He beckons.

"Kom binne," he says hospitably. "Come in."

Nathalie moves slowly towards him. The atmosphere is thick with menace. Or is it just the incongruity of an ageing, shabbily dressed man sitting at an ultra-modern desk?

"Captain Fuchs.," She clears her throat. "I have an appointment with Captain Fuchs," she says in Afrikaans.

"He's busy." He draws out a chair from behind the desk. "Sit maar," he says. "He won't be long."

He glances at the newspaper and shakes his head.

"What is this world coming to," he says. "Everywhere there's unrest, murder, revolution. Only here is there peace and stability."

She smiles at him, shakily. He smiles back and continues reading.

"Nice switchboard, nê?"

She had been looking at the six disks set into a metal plate on the desk.

"Very clever buttons. But you got to be very careful how you use them."

She offers him a cigarette. The room is bare, except for the desk and two chairs. To her left is a corridor to which the old man had pointed when he said Captain Fuchs was busy.

"What do these clever buttons do?" she asks.

"You speak Afrikaans so nicely."

"I grew up in a small country town and went to an Afrikaans medium school."

"Yes, the buttons. Let's say some skelm, someone with bad intentions, comes into this office without permission. All I do is press one of these buttons, and an iron door will jump out of that wall and shut off the corridor from this room."

"Very clever, Oom. But if this skelm gets a fright and wants to escape, he can rush back into the lift. There's nobody to stop him till he reaches the ground floor. I didn't see a soul when I came in. The lift goes straight down, doesn't it?"

"Ag man, we know these skelms' tricks. All I do is press another button and the lift will stop. He can't get out. If I'm too slow and he reaches the ground floor, I press another button and the doors won't open. By that time I've rung the alarm and our boys arrive. I press button number four and the lift comes right back to this room. The doors open and he's in for big trouble."

"Is this the top floor?" Nathalie feels chilled. Perhaps it's the air-conditioning.

"Everything you want to know, meisie! How do they say it, curiosity kills the bird in the hand. But yes, there's another floor. That's where the real skelms are persuaded to tell you interesting things. When they're asked nicely." He chuckles.

She hears a light tread in the corridor. A tall, slim man with broad shoulders is walking towards them. The Special Branch character in Bernard's novel isn't a Hollywood stereotype after all. He had used her description of Fuchs and churned it into fiction. With his tanned face and short blond hair, Fuchs could also be cast as a ski instructor in the Austrian Alps. Except for those icy blue eyes.

"I see Oupa de Jong has been entertaining you." Oupa wilts under his glare. Fuchs looks down at Nathalie with a smile that doesn't reach his eyes. "Come through to my office, Mrs Cohn."

His office is cold, inhospitable: white walls, a metal filing cabinet, two chairs and a large desk on which neat piles of papers and files cover half the surface. The dark carpet gives off an unpleasant smell of glue and sisal.

"So, Mrs Cohn, what can we do for you?"

"I've come about Miss Fletcher, Judith Fletcher," she says, keeping her voice steady. He's probably trained to recognise nervous symptoms. "When she's released, she'll need a place …"

"And you're offering to accommodate her."

"Not exactly. I have difficulties."

"What kind?"

"It's my father." She smiles in what she hopes is not an ingratiating manner. "He, well, he has a morbid hatred of communism. He'd be terribly upset if Judith, Miss Fletcher, came to stay with me. Especially if she were under constant surveillance, house arrest and all that."

"I see. He doesn't like us either."

"He doesn't want anything to do with politics."

"Is having Fletcher in your home a political act?"

"When the Soviet Union annexed Latvia in 1940," she says, "my father was deported to a labour camp in Siberia. He was to have joined us on the next ship, but there wasn't another ship. He escaped from Siberia after the war, and made his way to us, here."

"Then I suppose Helen Klein will have her. She and Fletcher were such good friends. Before Miss Klein made that statement, to please us. I was expecting her this afternoon."

"She's teaching."

"I hear she's a clever woman. In her field. Have you noticed," he leans forward confidentially, "how unattractive most political women are? Especially those on the left. On appearance alone I'd trust you. Will she take Fletcher in?"

Nathalie is confused by his abrupt change from the personal to the cool, direct question.

"Not exactly. That is, if she's not to be house-arrested, we could share it."

"That, Mrs Cohn, is irrelevant. All we need to know is where she's to live when she's released."

"I ask about house arrest because that's the crux of my problem. My father visits on weekends. He needn't know Miss Fletcher is staying with me if she could go to Helen Klein for the weekends. She can have Miss Fletcher only if she's not house-arrested."

"Fletcher must remain in one place. I believe her parents won't have her either. There is bad feeling between them."

They're tapping her phone, and he doesn't care if she knows it.

"I'm sure you've read the court proceedings, so you know Fletcher's coffee table was bugged," he continues. Nathalie's beginning to understand why people under pressure jump from tenth floor windows. "We trust you, Mrs Cohn, because we know from certain conversations you had with Fletcher that you do not sympathise with her ideas."

She wishes she had the guts to say, stop calling her Fletcher.

"We know you're good friends, and that's why it would be convenient if she stayed with you. We trust you."

Nathalie smarts at the compliment.

"I've explained about my father."

"He might be able to drum some sense into Fletcher's head. She's as intractable now as she's ever been. She's learned nothing from her experience in jail. Interesting," he continues when she doesn't answer. "Fletcher and her friends always take the moral high ground. We're the villains and they're out to save the world. Now Fletcher's a thorn in their flesh as well.

She's got lots of comrades, it seems, but few friends. Well, if neither you nor Miss Klein will have her, we'll give her a permanent address in a boarding house in Braamfontein. That's where we send released vagrants, prostitutes and other offenders."

He's enjoying her humiliation. Risking another snub Nathalie says, "If only I knew whether or not she's to be house-arrested ..."

"That's not up for discussion. All she needs is a permanent address."

"I might be able to furnish one," she says after a short silence. "A friend of mine who understands my difficulties may accommodate Miss Fletcher." He raises his eyebrows in genuine surprise. "She has a large house, is politically uninvolved, and does not know Judith very well."

"Why would she take her in? Does she sympathise with Fletcher's views?"

I don't know! Nathalie wants to yell. She's just a sentimental fool who can't bear to see people suffer, so unscrupulous friends take advantage of her.

"She's the sort of person who takes in stray dogs," she blurts out.

"An interesting analogy." He takes out a gold-nibbed pen from his breast pocket.

Nathalie looks at the cut of his suit. A natty dresser. And incredibly vain. She's heard stories of how he manipulates the emotions of women in solitary confinement. A music graduate from a well-known Cape university, it is rumoured he whistles arias from Wagner's operas while sitting in on interrogations.

How can she face Miriam? All she'd offered was to speak to Bernard. On the other hand, it might shake

Miriam out of her ivory tower. And if Bernard thinks Judith's so intelligent, they can spend the evenings in intellectual discussion.

"Name?" Fuchs asks.

"Nathanson. Miriam Nathanson."

"Nathanson? Rings a bell." He writes down the address.

"Good of you to call." He replaces the pen in his breast pocket. "That's what I appreciate about you. You don't wait for us to call on you."

She does not look at him as they walk towards the lift.

"Totsiens!" Oupa de Jong says. "I'll give you a nice ride down." His hand hovers over his switchboard.

Fuchs nods curtly. The doors shut and the lift goes down. She retraces her way to the main vestibule where another group of manacled prisoners is muddying the floor. The cleaner stands to one side, leaning on his mop. A Herculean labour, cleaning out the stables.

2

As her mother's car noses up the drive, Miriam wonders what storm she will unleash this afternoon; the air crackles with gale warnings. Molly Goldin bangs her door shut, and moves around to help Uncle Ben out of the car. He waves her aside. "Don't treat me like an invalid!" he splutters. Edging himself out of the seat, he leans against the door, his shoulders heaving as he fights for breath. Molly shrugs, gathers up her bag and hat from the back seat, and strides towards the house.

She is taller and slimmer than Miriam, better groomed, and every inch the chairwoman of half a dozen committees. Presidential.

"He becomes more impossible by the day," she hisses as she brushes past Miriam. "And you look positively dowdy. Have your hair done and buy yourself a new dress. I'll pay if you can't afford it."

Miriam hurries over to Ben and gives him her arm. "How are you, Ben?"

"Old people shouldn't be born," he gasps. "And that mother of yours is a tiger. Just because she controls the purse strings, she thinks she owns your soul. Wait till I tell you what happened on Monday."

"I know what happened on Monday."

"So, aren't I right?" Ben demands. "Jack's an idiot. He doesn't know what's happening in the world. He thinks Oslo is the capital of Holland."

"Jack's a kind man," Miriam says firmly.

Since Ben had given up his dingy one-roomed flat in the city two years ago, he has been living with Tillie, his younger sister, her husband Jack and their daughter Rita. Ben is fond of Tillie, but cannot bear Jack, a droopy-eyed, good-natured man who, Ben told Molly, takes little interest in anything but eating, sleeping, and the state of his digestion. And his daughter's the same, he added. Some diet she's on. First she eats her diet, then she has dinner. Molly had lashed out fiercely at him. He eats his own, she told him, and if not for them, you'd be sitting around in the Aged Home with other chronically ill people, waiting to die.

Omitting the reason for his argument with Molly, Ben complained to Tillie. She's always reminding me of my debt to both of you, he said. Tillie, a large, soft-hearted woman, who has often been humiliated by Molly, had phoned her immediately. It's unforgivable to remind a sick man of his dependence on us, she said angrily. Do you know what he said? Molly thundered. It doesn't matter, Tillie responded. He has a right to his opinions. Had Molly not been faced with the prospect of taking Ben into her own elegant flat, she'd have told Tillie exactly what Ben had said. As it was, she boiled inwardly but said nothing. But Ben had felt the full force of her fury.

Miriam can barely feel Uncle Ben's weight on her arm. A faint smell of the sickroom clings to him, evoking the row of medicine bottles on his bedside table, and an oxygen tank behind the bed-head. There had been other rooms, smoke-filled and stuffy, in which he had wasted away his life, gambling through the night, eating little and smoking too much, until his lungs had been reduced to useless sponge. He had been very good-looking as a young man. Now his large brown eyes have sunk deeply into their sockets, his thin, straight nose is pinched and pale, and his skin is drawn tightly over his skull, exposing the vein that ticks at his temple.

Miriam settles him into a comfortable armchair and puts on his favourite record, Russian folk songs performed by the Soviet Army Ensemble. The songs remind him of his childhood in the old country. He sits back, closes his eyes and smiles. Molly had immigrated to South Africa twelve years before Ben and Tillie, and preferred not to think about the Eastern European village of her childhood. Her siblings speak English with a distinct Yiddish accent; she slurs her r's slightly.

"I'll make tea," Molly says.

"Ben," Miriam whispers when her mother leaves the room, "I've got a problem. I know you'll understand. I remember the books and journals you used to read ..."

"Miriam! What have you been up to?"

"Relax." She laughs. "You know I'm not a political activist. Someone I know is coming out of jail on Thursday and she has no place to go. Her family lives in the Eastern Cape, her friends are either in jail or in exile, and those who're around, well, I suppose they don't want to get involved."

"You're looking for trouble, Miriam. Wait till your mother finds out."

"That's the point. I have to tell her today. If she finds out from someone else, she'll never speak to me again."

"She'll speak to you all right, like she spoke to me the other day."

As Miriam stands up to turn the record over, a car pulls up in the driveway. "It's too late, Ben! They're here!"

The front doors of the car open simultaneously, and

two dark-suited men emerge, one tall and dark, the other short and fair. Her heart thumps against her ribs. It is only three days since she'd agreed to have Judith, and here they are, coming to interrogate them. Neither she nor Bernard has removed any of the books or papers from the study, and his manuscript lies open on the desk.

"Ben," she turns off the radiogram, "please try to keep Ma out of the lounge. Tell her salesmen have called, anything, only keep her away."

Ben looks puzzled. She points to the window. He struggles to his feet and moves laboriously towards the kitchen.

Miriam reaches the front door before they ring the bell.

"Pretend you're salesmen for the Encyclopaedia Britannica," she whispers as the taller of the two puts out his hand and says, "I'm Lieutenant Van As from the …" The men stare at her.

"It's my mother," she whispers. "She's got a thing about policemen. This is a bad time to have called."

The dogs streak across the lawn, barking wildly.

"Silly clots!" She smacks Zorba as he lunges towards the Lieutenant. Bouboulina slinks away, growling. "Very protective of me," she smiles distractedly. "Strays, actually. That is, their mother was a stray before she died. After she gave birth to six puppies, in Bernard's wardrobe, of all places. And he's so finicky …"

"May we come inside? You are Mrs Nathanson, aren't you?" Van As asks. Miriam retreats a little, holding the door half open.

"Of course. Come in. But if my mother comes into the room, please pretend you're selling encyclopaedias. She'll have a fit if she hears you're policemen."

"Sure. Sorry for intruding, but we have something urgent to discuss with you, otherwise we'd come back another day."

"I didn't catch your name," she says to the second man as she leads them into the lounge. Always get their names, Bernard had coached her. He had oiled-down frizzy hair, parted in the centre, and his lips were pursed under his thin, dark moustache. He was not enjoying his role as a salesman of encyclopaedias.

"Sergeant Smit," he says, looking at her sternly. He must be the tough one. They work in pairs, she'd heard. One did the torturing, the other the comforting.

Van As looks like a preacher. There is a distinct Sunday night quality in his soft voice. She can imagine him casting his eyes Heavenwards: Come, let us pray … Or more likely, Repent, ye sinners.

"We won't keep you long," Van As says as she looks anxiously towards the kitchen. "Just a few routine questions. We have to do this before Miss Fletcher comes to live here."

"Not that chair!" she cries as he is about to lower himself on to the straight-backed chair with ball and claw legs.

He jumps up and looks down at the chair.

"Sorry." She suppresses a nervous giggle. "That's my mother's chair. My husband Bernard calls it her throne. She's got a bad back and has to sit on a straight-backed chair. Try this one. Much more comfortable."

He sits down cautiously and takes out his pen and notebook. Miriam sits on the edge of her chair. No mention of a search yet. Miriam's mouth is dry and her palms are sweating.

"Pity you didn't let me know you were coming. I'd have kept my mother away."

"We're informal people. We like to drop in unexpectedly." Van As smiles. "How did you know we'd be coming?"

"I was told you usually come to, uh, inspect the premises."

"True. We like to know our charges will be comfortable."

The charm will evaporate when he finds those books. His round, open face and receding hairline give him a benign look, but his lips are twisted into a thin smile which she does not find reassuring: this man can be cruel. She wonders if she should offer them coffee. It seems important to either offer them coffee or not: it establishes the kind of relationship you're setting up. No. She will not offer them coffee. She hopes Bernard returns before they search his study.

The first questions are innocuous enough: How many people live in the house; what is her full name, her husband's name, her children's names and ages. How many servants live on the premises, their names. What her husband does for a living, and how many rooms there are in the house. Would Judith have a room to herself, he asks finally.

Perhaps, after all, they are concerned for her comfort.

She catches Sergeant Smit's eye and follows it to the carpet. The cover of the record she had been playing for Ben lies face upwards: Emblazoned across the top of the cover in large black letters is "The Soviet Army Ensemble". Beneath the title is a picture of about fifty Russians soldiers in uniform, their mouths formed into O's. The backdrop is a red curtain. At each end of the stage hangs a red flag with a hammer, a sickle and a star in the right-hand corner. Her glance meets the Sergeant's just above the record cover.

Her mother appears in the doorway. She stands there uncertainly for a while, glancing from Miriam to the two men. The Lieutenant surreptitiously slips his notebook into his pocket and smiles at Miriam.

"So you see," Miriam says, too loudly. "We already have an edition of the encyclopaedia, though it's an old one. Quite useless for Scrabble. The other night my husband was looking for the name of a bird which he claims lives in a South American jungle. He couldn't find it. Perhaps it hadn't evolved by 1928, he remarked, rather wittily, don't you think?"

Her mother hovers around the door for a few more seconds, then disappears.

"You did that very well." Van As looks at Miriam carefully.

Too well. Now he knows I'm a liar. Why am I so agitated? I really must think before I blurt out stupid things. If only my mother would stay away.

"You don't share your mother's view of us, do you?" he asks.

"No. At least, this is the first time I've met you, but I'm sure you're perfectly nice people. You see, my mother has an Eastern European background and is suspicious of anything to do with political movements, police or jails."

"We're not monsters, you know." She'd heard of their desire to be loved while doing their duty. "We're just ordinary human beings, doing an ordinary job. If we didn't do our work properly, people like your mother wouldn't sleep peacefully at night."

"I'm sure you're very good at your job."

"Certain people," he says in an aggrieved tone, "and you'll be meeting one of them soon enough, will tell you otherwise. But Miss Fletcher will find out that if she does what she's supposed to do, she won't have any trouble from us. She probably expects us to be sitting on your doorstep ..."

"And will you be?"

"We have more important things to do, Mrs Nathanson."

"I'm sure you have."

"It's a good thing Fletcher will be living with a sensible woman like you," he says. Now I'm his accomplice. "Perhaps you'll show her the error of her ways." The preacher again. "I've had long chats with her, but she's very obstinate. An unyielding woman who's learned nothing from her experiences. Where do you know her from, Mrs Nathanson?"

"She's a friend of my friend, Mrs Cohn. I don't know her very well, but Mrs Cohn couldn't have her for family reasons, so I said she could come to us."

"Have you ever belonged to a political party?"

"Well, yes." She hesitates. He smiles, encouraging her to continue. "I've been a member of the Women's Zionist League for the last ten years. But I'm not very active. I make marmalade and wholewheat bread for their annual morning market."

"Very good marmalade, I'm sure. But if I know Fletcher, you'll be having interesting discussions about politics, South African politics."

"I'm sure Miss Fletcher will not wish to discuss politics with us," she answers primly.

"What do your children feel about your taking in a virtual stranger?"

"My children," Miriam sits up very straight, "never question my hospitality." The longer she knows him, the less she likes him.

"What school do they go to?"

Miriam tells him.

"Ah, the Jewish school. We've had trouble with several members on the staff. What do you think about Zionism, Mrs Nathanson?"

"I believe we should have our own homeland."

"But you wouldn't like to live there yourself, would you? South Africa's an easy, peaceful place to live in, isn't it?"

"South Africa is one of the most beautiful countries in the world."

"The only trouble," he says, looking down at the record cover on the floor, "is that it's becoming too cosmopolitan. That record, Mrs Nathanson. Are you fond of Russian music?"

"That record is a particular favourite of my uncle's. He's also visiting me at the moment."

"Was he born in Russia?"

"In Lithuania."

"And you? Were you born in South Africa?"

"Ja. I've lived here all my life."

Why hadn't she thrust the damn record cover under a cushion when she saw them coming? A fuller explanation is required. She picks up the cover and walks over to the Lieutenant.

"Do you know any of these songs? They're often requested on the Afrikaans programme of the South African Broadcasting Corporation. Kalinka and Volga Boatman are great favourites. I wouldn't be surprised if they came from this particular record."

"I don't know much about music. I'm a strictly tikkie-draai man myself, very keen on our folk music. And hymns of course. I'm a deacon of my church."

Molly appears at the door again.

"Won't be long, Ma," she calls. "The gentlemen are just leaving." The men stand up and her mother goes away.

"Thanks, Mrs Nathanson. That'll be all." Lieutenant Van As puts away his notebook.

Miriam sighs. The search, it seems, is put off for another day. "There's something I'd like to ask," she says. "How will all this affect my husband and children? We've lived a very quiet life and I'd not welcome disruptions."

"As long as you don't aid and abet Miss Fletcher to break her bans, you'll be left entirely alone."

"Bans? What bans?"

"Fletcher, Miss Fletcher, will be informed about these before she comes to you. She'll be confined to your magisterial area. She'll have to report daily to your nearest police station. She must be confined to your house between six in the evening until seven next morning. On Saturdays she must not leave the house after two in the afternoon until seven on Monday morning. And she may not mix with your visitors. Two's a company, like they say. Three can land her in jail for a year. It is very generous of you to have her, Mrs Nathanson, and we hope she won't make life difficult for you. If she does, you must consider it your duty to inform us immediately. Your family comes before a stranger, not so, Mrs Nathanson? We wouldn't want you to get into trouble on her account."

The blood drains from Miriam's face. Not only is she being threatened; they also expect her to be an informer. A few days ago she had frivolously imagined herself as a warder in this suburban prison. Now it is a reality.

At the door Van As shakes hands with her and says in a loud voice, "If you decide to buy the encyclopaedia, Ma'am, please contact me at my office."

He is clearly delighted with his performance.

With a nod and a clammy handshake, Sergeant Smit takes leave of her. She wipes her hand surreptitiously against her dress and waits for them to drive away before she returns to the lounge. Uncle Ben catches her eye and shrugs helplessly. Her mother sits in her chair, straight-backed, a thunderbolt in each hand.

"Those men," she begins quietly enough, "are policemen." The word "policemen" seems to oil her anger. "Encyclopaedia salesmen indeed! How dare you put on such an act, together with them. What do you think I am? A senile idiot? I heard them speak about banning orders. Who's coming to live here? I want the truth!"

"Judith Fletcher."

"Are you off your head? You'll be locked up! And don't expect me to look after your horde when you've gone. Taking in a jailbird ... Don't you dare shout at me! I know what I'm saying. People don't go to jail for nothing. How can you even consider it? A criminal, a communist, someone you don't even know. I shall not put my foot in your house until this person has left. And look how you've upset Ben with your hysterical shouting. You'll be the death of us all. Quick! Bring him a glass of water! He's white as a sheet and can't catch his breath. And if Bernard allows you to do this, he's a bigger fool than I thought ..."

"Leave her alone!" Ben summons what air is left in his lungs. "She's doing what any feeling human being should do!"

Molly Goldin stares at her brother, picks up her bag, and hustles him out of the house.

"You'll not see me until your guest has come and gone," she shouts, reversing the car out of the drive.

"Promise?" Miriam whispers. This time she has Bernard on her side. She sinks onto the garden swing and starts planning the menu for the first dinner with their guest.

3

The heavy wooden door closes behind her. She is free. But when the peep-hole slides open, then shuts with a snap, she feels the old familiar panic. Will they never stop watching her? She takes a deep breath, picks up her suitcase, and walks slowly down the steps between two rows of black men and women. No one responds to her smile. They stand huddled in the cold morning air, clutching parcels wrapped in newspaper, cartons of milk, loaves of bread. They have a long wait ahead; visiting time is two hours away.

She looks around in bewilderment. The Fort stands on a high point, overlooking the jagged skyline of the city. Many old landmarks are dwarfed by new structures over which enormous cranes hover. The sky is full of movement. On her return from England, seven years ago, the city had looked smaller and dingier, a provincial backwater. After living in confined spaces for three years, it seems like a thriving metropolis. To her right, where once a road led down to the University, a corrugated iron fence closes off excavations. A builder's board announces the site of a new civic centre. She used to walk along that road to University, between rows of semi-detached houses, past grubby children, barking dogs and women with curlers in their hair. All gone.

The early morning sun reflects off the sleek, shiny surfaces of cars, blinding her. She will need sunglasses. Behind tinted lenses the world might not look so threatening. A young student on his way to University greets her, and she is drawn into contact with the world again. He takes the detour around the excavations, and she walks in the other direction, towards Hillbrow.

The raw spring breeze carries the smell of blossoms over the high walls of the Chief Warder's house. She touches the rough bark of a plane tree, marvelling at its resilience. Defying the rings of concrete that cramp its growth, it still puts out leaves in spring.

She'd lain awake in her cell all night, listening to the sounds of the city: the chugging of a distant train, the roar of motor cycles, cars changing gear up Hospital Hill. Several times she was woken by the sirens of ambulances as they drew up at the Non-European Hospital opposite the Fort, the Fever Hospital on its left, and the General Hospital several blocks away. One expects to hear sirens on Hospital Hill, yet every wail set off waves of anxiety. It was dawn before she fell asleep.

Her cell was identical to the one in which she had spent five weeks before and during her trial. There was just enough space for a bed, a tiny locker and a sanitary bucket at the foot of the bed. The large, barred sash window that looked onto the courtyard made the cramped space bearable. A cell with a view. Unlike that dank, evil-smelling cell in the police station outside Pretoria where she had spent fifty-eight days in solitary confinement. She had torn her finger nails trying to reach the high, barred and netted window that looked onto the exercise yard.

During those months of interminable interrogation, she had learned to handle the verbal abuse and humiliation to which her interrogators had subjected her. She sat on her hands to hide the trembling, trying to look impassive and calm, but she never lost her fear of physical torture. There was a point, she had heard, beyond which one would say anything to stop the torture. When Lieutenant Van As walked triumphantly into the interrogation room one day, she knew someone had cracked. You might as well make a statement, he said. Ralph Ferguson has told us everything. She could barely disguise her shock. He was lying, of course. Interrogators lied to extract confessions. He's a special friend of yours, isn't he, Van As mocked, using Ralph's term of endearment for her. Shortly afterwards she was transferred to the Fort. She spent the weeks awaiting trial at the barred sash window, drawing into her numbed body what little warmth was to be had from the winter sun.

She crosses the street at the traffic light. The Fort is behind her. To survive, to remain sane, she must root herself firmly in the present. She is apprehensive of moving in on the Nathansons who are relative strangers. But there's no place else she can go. Her parents won't have her, most of her friends are either in jail or in exile, Helen is planning to go overseas, and Nathalie has problems with her father.

Her banning orders are harsh. She will not be permitted to teach in a school where, presumably, she would pollute the minds of innocent children with the rules of English grammar. She has no other training. Vanguard Booksellers in the city are known to employ political ex-prisoners but, as the Nathansons live in the peri-urban area, she will not be allowed to work in the city. No more decisions for now. She has several hours in which to relish her brief, untrammelled freedom.

On a street corner she lingers over the English and Afrikaans papers laid out on the pavement with small piles of coins beside them. Accessibility of newspapers had become an obsession in jail. Except for an occasional article in one of the women's magazines which had not been censored, she has little idea of what was happening in the world. An uncensored sentence in one of Nathalie's letters, has remained a mystery.

"Where's Biafra?" she had asked her cell-mates.

She walks into a large pharmacy opposite the hospital for her next purchase, a pair of sunglasses. She draws in a deep breath. Pharmacies these days smell nothing like those of her childhood — medicinal, antiseptic. A wonderful smell of soap, perfume and powder fills the shop. The shelves are laden with pottery, wooden bowls, copper vases and kitchenware in bright oranges, blues and greens. She's almost forgotten such things exist. A large stand displays a variety of sunglasses. She tries on a pair which cost twice as much as her monthly chemist's allowance in jail. Prison-issue toothpowder had made her gag, and the red soap was fat and greasy. Small wonder we're regarded as spoiled white ladies, her fellow prisoners had said when they ordered their own toothpaste, soap and sanitary towels. Black prisoners could not afford such luxuries.

"Have you any cheaper glasses?" she asks the miniskirted assistant. Her voice sounds unfamiliar to her.

"This is our cheapest line," the assistant says briskly. "Try the bazaars."

Adjustment number one: she can't afford sunglasses from glossy pharmacies. The previous evening she had worked out her budget. Out of a total of three hundred rand, the remains of her last salary cheque, she has to keep herself until she finds a job. She can make do with the clothes she has, but will have to shorten all her dresses and skirts. Not as short as the pharmacy assistant's, who, when she leans over, reveals a large section of upper thigh.

The streets are filling up with people on their way to work. Her haziness and anxiety begin to wear off as she walks unnoticed among the crowds. She catches a glimpse of herself in a shop window. Her old fashioned suit hangs loosely from her shoulders, and her skirt is well below the knee. Her blonde hair has become dull and lifeless, streaked with grey. She has paid in years for the highlights in her hair.

At the OK Bazaar she buys a pair of cheap sunglasses. I have a pair like that myself, the saleslady tells her. Next stop is the tobacconist where she buys several packs of cigarettes. She'd become expert at rolling her own cigarettes, enjoying the bite brown-paper gives to pipe tobacco. She lights a cigarette, inhaling deeply. Easy to get used to luxury. With her glasses, newspaper and cigarettes, she is equipped to make her long-awaited pilgrimage to the Florian.

She had dreamed of sitting on the balcony of the café, in the sun. She even planned what she'd order. In the general bleakness of prison life, swamped by deprivations of every kind, her emotional life had become centred around food. Because so much of her life had been tied up with the café, she had forgotten what indifferent food it served. You went to the Florian primarily to meet friends, to kibbitz over a game of chess, to look at and listen to other people. In prison the fantasised meals had glowed with culinary genius.

About a block from the café, she stops and looks into the window of a music shop. With the sixth sense she has developed over the years, she knows she is being followed. She turns her head casually from the window in the direction from which she has come. For a moment she sees only the milling crowds. Then she picks out a tall young man in a navy blue suit, standing at the cinema, about thirty feet away, examining the stills of the forthcoming film. Her mouth goes dry and her knees begin to tremble. What purpose is there in tailing her on the first morning of her release? Where can she run? What can she communicate, and to whom? She hurries towards the café, her exuberant mood dampened. Before she walks into the Florian, she turns again. The young man is nowhere to be seen. He's probably in the cinema, watching a film. Beware of paranoia, friends had warned.

A warm vanilla smell draws her into Florian's cake shop; the café itself is upstairs. The display counter is exactly as she remembers it, with its abundance of almond tarts, cheese cakes, yeast buns, Danish pastries and an assortment of biscuits. At the far end of the counter stands Mrs Lonsdale, the elderly woman who used to keep an almond tart for her on Friday evenings.

"Miss Fletcher!" she calls out happily. "My dear Miss Fletcher! Where have you been all this time? Not overseas again? How naughty of you not to say goodbye. But you're so thin, my dear. And so pale. Not much sun over there, I suppose."

She responds gratefully to Mrs Londsale's warm hug. Is it possible she doesn't know? The trial, she'd heard, had been splashed over all the newspapers.

"Indeed, Mrs Lonsdale, I've been away."

"I'm so pleased to see you again. You'll tell me all about it later. Go upstairs for a nice cuppa."

"May I leave my suitcase with you for a while?"

"As long as there're no bombs in it." Mrs Lonsdale laughs. "I'll keep it behind the counter. Goodness, you travel light. When I go to Durban for a long weekend, I take more than that with me."

She walks up the familiar stone stairs. The first five feet of wall are panelled with wood, the rest is wall-papered. At the top of the stairs are two green doors, one marked "Ladies", the other "Gentlemen".

Through the east windows, the sun streams into the café, casting a pale light on five rows of ceramic-tiled tables. As always, she averts her eyes from the stuffed antelope's head that glares down balefully on the empty room. A few people are having breakfast on the balcony.

May the Florian, shabby though it is, never be demolished. She walks towards the balcony. Two elderly women are having tea with cream scones. At separate tables, three men are reading their newspaper while they eat. She recognises none of them.

The tables in the direct sun are unoccupied. She sits down, facing onto Twist Street. Like the other tables, it is weather-worn, the plastic chairs are faded and brittle, and the ashtrays are dented.

"Good morning, Miss Fletcher," a deep African voice says at her side. "What will you have for breakfast?"

"Iphraim!" She stretches out her hand. He averts his eyes and she drops it onto her lap. "How nice to see you again."

"How is Miss Fletcher?" He looks at her carefully. "You've been away a long time."

"I'm better now, thank you. How is Phillip?"

Phillip is his only son. She had taught him at night school several years ago. He should be writing his matriculation exam at the end of the year.

"Phillip was arrested five months ago. Tsotsis chased him one night on his way back from school. He jumped into a car in a driveway, to hide. The tsosis ran past him, but the boss came out of the house. Phillip was arrested for trying to steal the car. He got eighteen months."

"Didn't he have a lawyer?"

"It didn't help, Ma'am. It was Phillip's word against the white man's."

She looks down at the sugar bowl Iphraim has placed at the centre of the table.

"Hey boy! Waiter! My bill!" one of the men calls out, snapping his fingers.

Nothing changes. Over the road yet another building is going up. She cannot remember what used to stand there. Cranes swing precariously across the busy street, and white foremen direct black workers. Beneath the surface prosperity, the delirious construction, and the busy, bustling crowds, Johannesburg is the same as ever, drawing everything sane and wholesome into its greedy maws.

"The same, Miss Fletcher?" Iphraim asks when he returns to her table.

"I've forgotten what 'the same' is, Iphraim."

"A glass of milk with anchovy toast, Ma'am."

"Let's be different today. I'll have toasted cheese and a cup of real coffee. The coffee at my hotel was terrible. Ground beetles, I think."

"Phillip says they don't get coffee."

"I know, Iphraim, I know."

She sits in the sun for two hours. By the time she's ready to leave, she feels warmed through and slightly lethargic. She leaves her newspaper on the table. She has read everything, including many of the advertisements. She picks up her handbag and says goodbye to

Iphraim. As she steps inside, she sees the tall young man in the navy blue suit, sitting at a table under the stuffed antelope, reading a newspaper.

Her heart beating rapidly, she goes downstairs to the public phone. With shaking fingers, she dials Nathalie's number.

"Nathalie? I'm at the Florian. Half-an-hour? Good. I'll wait at the bus stop."

"Slegs vir Blankes". Every municipal bench bears that legend, in English and in Afrikaans. Judith moves away from the bus stop, declining the honour of sitting on a bench for whites only. She leans against a pillar outside the Florian. Soon she will be at the Nathansons, a stranger at their table, but she will accept the Nathanson's hospitality with as much grace as she can muster; an uneasy guest is a burden.

"You look like a stork, standing against that pillar on one leg," Nathalie calls as she draws up. Judith rushes to the car and embraces her. There is much to talk about and before they realise it, they have left the bustle of Hillbrow. As they approach the Wilds, Judith looks across the leafy suburbs towards the vast veld which stretches away towards the purple hills of the Magaliesberg range. They wind down the valley of the Wilds, into the tree-lined streets where jacarandas show the first hint of lilac.

"I'd forgotten how beautiful it is," Judith murmurs. "But I'm nervous ..."

"You'll get on well with the Nathansons. Miriam's a little scatty but very kind, and Bernard is only formidable if you don't know him. In no time at all, he'll have captured your soul in his little black book and transformed you from a person into a character."

"How ghoulish!"

"I can't imagine why he thinks you're intelligent. If you were, you'd have skipped the country before they caught you. And if you have any common sense at all, you'll move out of hostile territory as soon as possible."

"I shall. Just as soon as I've caught my breath."

"Seriously, Judith. Apply immediately for your exit permit, and for permission to enter Britain. These things take time. If you remain in this country, you'll be a perpetual prisoner. They'll never lift your bans. But come the Revolution ..."

"I may be dead by then."

"Judith! They've knocked the spirit out of you."

"No. Everything I've experienced over the last three years has confirmed me in my beliefs. It's the present I'm concerned with. Is old Crouse still chief archivist at the Daily Mail? I need to dredge up the lost years. Ask him to lend me a few newspaper files at a time."

"You know he can't ..."

"He's your pal. The sooner I catch up with the last three years, the sooner I'll leave. I promise."

"I'll ask him. Writing a book or what?"

"Every ex-prisoner, every exile has a book in her."

"Before we get to the Nathansons, let's book you in at the police station where you'll be reporting every day."

They drive through farmlands and veld, skirting the highway to the airport. The fields are brown and dry with winter grass and khaki weed. Passing a smallholding, Judith at last sees the blossoms she had imagined in Hillbrow, great clouds of pink and white blossoms. She opens her window, breathing in the honeyed scent, and with it, the smell of rain in the dust-filled air. Thunder clouds are gathering over the hills.

They drive into the grounds of an old school building, much like the one Judith had herself attended: red-bricked, L-shaped, with sash windows. Behind the main building are two corrugated iron cells with tiny netted windows. Near the drive, two unsupervised black prisoners in red-and-white-striped shirts are digging a ditch. Nathalie parks in the quadrangle where the circles and rectangles of a hopscotch game are still visible.

The formality of signing on is lengthy; the sergeant has never dealt with what he calls a political case. Judith explains patiently that she will be coming to report every day between seven in the morning and six in the evening, and that the police station's register would probably be scrutinised periodically by the Security Police. The sergeant calls in the Captain when she mentions Security Police.

"Name, address?" the Captain asks brusquely as he takes out a large book from behind the wooden counter. He fill in the details, and pushes it towards Judith. "Sign there," he says. Judith signs.

"A sign of the times, excuse the pun," she says when they leave the office. "And they shall beat police stations out of primary school buildings." She drops a packet of cigarettes out of the window as they pass the two prisoners digging the ditch.

"You should see their new building in town. All concrete, steel and blue panelling. Remind me to tell you about my interview with Captain Fuchs when we're both feeling stronger."

4

"Why has she been in jail?" Willie asks Miriam, putting down his comic book. Pippa and Henry are lying on the carpet, playing draughts.

"She was against the Government." They should have been here by now.

"Yeh, but what did she do? Was she a spy? Did she kill someone?"

"Shut up, Willie," Henry says. "She didn't kill anyone. She broke some stupid laws. Your move, Pippa."

"They're here!" Miriam hurries to the door. "Call Dad from the study."

She hardly recognises Judith. Her face is pale and drawn, her smile uncertain, her eyes clouded. She looks frail in the unfashionable suit which hangs loosely from her shoulders.

"I'm so pleased you'll be staying with us." Miriam embraces her. "Come, meet the family. Henry, Pippa, William." The older two shake hands. William gazes at her with undisguised curiosity. "The oldest, Lawrence, is overseas with his class on a study tour."

"It's lovely to see children again," Judith says.

"It'll wear off. And don't feel obliged to answer Willie's questions. He doesn't know when to stop."

"I just want to know ..." William begins. Henry nudges him.

There is a relaxed, homely atmosphere in the lounge. A shaggy off-white carpet covers the floor, and the curtains are drawn to each side of a large picture window which faces onto a secluded garden bordered by pine trees. In the far corner of the room stands an open grand piano and behind it, on a ledge over the fireplace, is an enormous vase with almond blossoms. Judith averts her eyes from the burglar-proofed windows; like impaled birds, Nathalie had said. A smell of baking and roasting wafts in from the kitchen. Her stomach rumbles; it is hours since she has eaten.

Bernard comes into the room, smiling.

"Hello Nathalie. Welcome, Judith. I'm pleased to see you again."

"I really don't know what to say. It's so good of you …"

"Make yourself at home. This place is a madhouse, of course. If you ever need to escape, feel free to use my study. It's out of bounds to children, dogs and mothers-in-law. And not necessarily in that order. You've yet to meet my mother-in-law." He exchanges glances with Miriam.

Miriam frowns. "My mother," she says, "has threatened to stay away from the house while you're living with us. So I hope you'll be here for at least six months. It's nothing personal, of course. She's just a difficult woman."

"Oh Miriam, I'm so sorry. The last thing I want is to cause trouble." She turns to Nathalie. "Perhaps we could …"

"Don't even think about it," Miriam says. "A week's as long as she'll hold out without harassing me. Her bite is worse than her roar. Roar back if you can. That'll surprise her. You'll love my Uncle Ben, though. He's looking forward to meeting you. Come, I'll show you to your room."

Judith follows her down the passage into a fair-sized room, with a bed, a small table with a vase of sweetpeas on it, a desk, a chair and a built-in wardrobe. On the wall, above the bed, is a poster of a black man with a raised, clenched fist: The Future is Black, runs the legend. Interspersed with school photographs, rugby teams and cricket teams, are posters of Bob Dylan and Joan Baez.

"This is Lawrence's room. He'll only be back in December so you're not displacing anyone. You look tired, Judith. Rest a while. We'll have tea later."

Judith turns away as tears well up in her eyes. When she looks around, Miriam has gone. She sits on the bed, breathing deeply, stilling her palpitations. She should unpack but feels too tired to get up. She lies back and within minutes has fallen into a deep, unrestful sleep.

Hands and knees grazed and bleeding, sweat pouring down her forehead, she crawls through the tunnel. Voices echo all around, closing in on her. The air is fetid and she gags on the stench. The voices grow louder, bouncing off the walls, piercing her ears. Her arms and legs seize up and she cannot move another inch ...

Judith wrenches free of the dream. In her recurring nightmare, her pursuers never catch up with her, but she never reaches the end of the tunnel. She will only be free of the dream when she does. Four-thirty; she has slept for three hours. She gets off the bed and follows the sound of loud voices.

"I see no point, no point at all, in giving Henry lessons," a high-pitched male voice is shouting.

"Mr Liebgott, I mean Gottlieb, he is musical. It would be such a pity to stop now. I'll speak to him, I'll make him apologise ..."

Miriam is in the entrance hall with a short young man whose pale complexion is blotchy with rage.

"Mrs Nathan," he draws himself up, "it's no good. Henry has the temperament but not the talent of a Paderewsky. Good afternoon!"

He brushes past Miriam and walks rapidly out of the house. Henry, eating an apple tart, comes in with Bernard. Judith looks at them in hazy astonishment.

"I warned you it was a madhouse," Bernard says.

"Who was that extraordinary person?"

"Was, is right. That was Henry's music teacher," Miriam says. "Paderewsky decided he had to have an apple tart in the middle of his music lesson. That brought to a head something that's been brewing for months. You did that deliberately, Henry."

"I offered him an apple tart as well. Anyway, I'd rather have guitar lessons."

"Did you hear him?" Bernard takes Judith's arm and steers her into the lounge. "A natural phrase-maker ... the temperament but not the talent of a Paderewsky ... He's wasted on a rogue like Henry."

Judith sits down, dazed.

"Sorry we woke you," Miriam says.

"I feel such an idiot. I lay down for what I thought would be a few minutes, and slept all afternoon. Did Nathalie leave long ago? It was very rude of me. I hadn't slept well last night ..."

"She understands. You must be ravenous. Have a hot bath and we'll have an early dinner. Perhaps you'd like a game of Scrabble with Bernard afterwards?"

"In Barberton we played Scrabble every evening."

"Then you'll not want to play."

"On the contrary. We were bored with one another's vocabularies. It'll be a challenge to play Scrabble with Bernard."

"Marvellous." Miriam sighs. "My self-esteem drops every time I play with him. I've never beaten him. Would you like to bath now? I'll show you where the towels are."

Judith lies back in the bath, her eyes closed. The benison of hot water. This is more than a blessing; it's a purification. She's soaking out the prison filth from her pores, from the depths of her being. Small wonder so many religious rites centre around water. She prefers pagan practices and Roman steam baths to the cold water dipping of the Christians. Had she known the Nathansons better, she might have sung in the bath. The last time she sang had been in Pretoria Central. If you'd ever sung through the night before a hanging together with your fellow prisoners, you should never want to sing again. But you do.

Judith dresses in the new green skirt, white blouse and black embroidered panty-hose she had bought in Hillbrow after her visit to the Florian. Her hair, with the aid of a colour rinse, has regained some of its lustre, but the skin around her eyes is permanently pleated, and her mouth is bracketed between two deep lines. As long as the fissures in my mind don't show, she thinks as she walks into the lounge.

William is playing with the dogs on the carpet, Bernard is hidden behind a newspaper, and Miriam sits on the couch between Pippa and Henry, following the score of the Mozart piano concerto they are listening to.

"A picture of domestic harmony," Judith says.

Miriam beams. "You look lovely, Judith."

"Indeed you do," Bernard adds.

"It's a habit we cultivated in jail. You know, dressing for dinner in the jungle."

"Welcome to the jungle," Bernard says.

"You know what I mean."

"Joke, joke. What will you drink?"

"Gin and tonic, please."

At dinner, William looks around the table, and forming his grubby fist into a gun, he takes aim. "Rat-a-tat-atat," he drones, aiming at each person in turn.

"For goodness sake, William," Miriam protests. "Who do you think you're shooting?"

"I'm a Green Beret, like the ones in my comic, and I'm shooting all the commies in Vietnam."

"Miriam," Bernard breaks the embarrassed silence, "our William is obviously reading the wrong comics. We must put him on Prince Valium immediately."

"Personally I prefer Hagar the Horrible," Judith laughs, "but try Charlie Brown first."

"Do you really mind if I ask you questions about jail?" William asks. "Ma says I shouldn't."

"What would you like to know, William?"

"Lots. But I can't remember what just now."

"Was the food in jail awful?" Henry asks shyly. "You know, bread and water and all that?"

"No, just dull. Porridge and coffee in the morning, pork and vegetables in the afternoon, soup, bread and a little butter and jam in the evening. Day after day after day."

"Do you play any musical instrument?" he asks.

"No. But I love music."

"I'll play the guitar after supper," he offers.

Pippa, who had been quiet throughout the meal, sits next to Judith on the couch, watching her crochet.

"Ma promised to teach me, but she's never got time. Is it hard to crochet?"

"It's easy. I'll show you how to do it. I couldn't crochet at all before I went to jail. A friend taught me."

Henry plays folk songs on his guitar. "I could show you how, if you like," he offers Judith.

"He's graduated from disgraced pupil to teacher." Bernard picks up the newspaper. "Too much competition tonight. Scrabble begins in earnest tomorrow evening."

"They're usually in their rooms by eight, listening to their favourite radio serials," Miriam says after the children leave the room. "I hope their questions don't upset you, Judith."

"Not at all. Many ex-prisoners suffer from the Ancient Mariner syndrome. You fix your audience with a glittering eye and bore them to death about how you saved and soured milk and hung it in a bra from the window to make cream cheese. Or how you secretly fermented prunes and got drunk on prune wine. Some of those detained during the 1960 State of Emergency regaled people endlessly with such tales."

"The State of Emergency," Bernard says, "was before the introduction of the Ninety-Day Clause and solitary confinement. Going to jail then was a kind of initiation rite for white politicals. I knew a chap who felt slighted because the State didn't think him dangerous enough to lock up during the Emergency. For the blacks, of course, it was always different."

Judith sits up straight. What right has he to be sarcastic about white politicals? But what right has she to resent it?

"Some of those people are now serving long-term sentences," she says. "Going to jail is no longer an initiation rite, if it ever was."

Bernard flushes and lowers his head. Miriam fidgets. For someone who professes to value silence, Bernard has certainly got off to a bad start. He is talking too much, showing off.

Had she sounded too abrupt, too self-righteous? Judith wonders. Was she coming over as a member of an exclusive club whose prerogative it is to use words like "stretches" and "solitary", just as certain students had spoken about psycho, socio, and bibstuds?

"I hear they're going to demolish the Fort." Judith shifts to less controversial matters. "Build more high rises."

"Speculators have had their eyes on it for a long time." Bernard is relieved she has let him off lightly. "But recently it was declared a national monument."

"I'm all for demolishing it. Though the Fort isn't bad as jails go." She laughs, embarrassed. "Listen to the connossieur."

"How was it in Barberton?" Miriam asks.

"It looks on to green fields and one can see the mountains in the distance. But the Fort has larger windows. Barred, of course, but then so are the windows of suburbia."

"Indeed." Bernard gets up from the chair. "I'm off to bed. I have an early lecture tomorrow. Scrabble tomorrow evening, Judith, so prepare for battle."

Next afternoon, Bernard takes her for a walk up the hill behind the house.

"Johannesburg begins from that hill," he says, pointing to the third dome in the range of hills which stretches away to the west. "If you walk beyond that, you're breaking your ban."

To the north-east, wooded suburbs are spread around two adjoining golf courses. In the south, old mining suburbs cluster near yellow mine dumps. The city itself, like a beached ship, lies between two parallel chains of hills in the west, its jagged skyline outlined against the clear sky, the cranes suspended over unfinished constructions.

"I feel like Lot's wife, looking back at Sodom and Gemorrah," she says.

"For a political woman, you use a lot of biblical imagery."

"My childhood was misspent among holy bigots."

"I can imagine you, one day, marching around Trafalgar Square, enclosed by sandwich boards, calling out, Repent! Redemption is at hand! Human beings seem to regress into religious belief as they grow older. Or into political faith, which is just as dangerous."

"Perhaps." She would not be provoked into a political argument.

After Nathalie brought Judith the first instalment of newspaper files, Miriam decided to start practising the piano again. I needed something to get me going, she told Judith. Within days they'd developed a routine. Judith worked on the files, Miriam played the piano and when they were ready for a break, they drove to the police station to report. Nathalie had taken Judith once or twice, but as her visits to the house tailed off, Miriam took over. Helen had not yet been to see her.

When they had visitors, Judith ate in her room, joined often by either Pippa, Willie or Henry. The Clubroom, Bernard called it. Henry was teaching her to play the guitar, she was showing Pippa how to crochet, and William, who had given up Green Beret comics for Snoopy and Charlie Brown, would curl up at the foot of her bed and ask for stories. His curiosity about jail, once she had emphasised the boredom and its lack of glamour, was quickly sated. She drew on her memory of African myths and told him about the mantis who tried to catch the moon, the tortoise who outwitted the mongoose, and about the rain-bulls who bring thunder storms. When her memory gave out, she invented tales; he liked stories about animals. As she spoke, he drew pictures of tortoises, hares, spotted-necked otters and honey badgers.

Often, in the evening, Judith plays Scrabble with Bernard. He plays competitively, creating a closed game; Judith is concerned with building words. He is surprised at the generosity with which she creates openings on the board.

"You lack aggression," he says, putting down a seven-letter word, "the urge to win."

"I've lots of aggression," she says, "but I have to find the right target for it. Before my arrest I went to Judo classes. I was the despair of my instructor. I couldn't throw my opponents unless I could conjure up a face I hated. He suggested I take up embroidery instead."

She had been with the Nathansons about two weeks, when Nathalie arrived with the second instalment of newspapers.

"You're getting too comfortable," she says when she finds Judith on the garden swing, telling William stories. "Just because Van As and his fellow asses haven't been harassing you, doesn't mean they're not out to get you. You must start applying for visas, booking a berth and so on. And this vicarious family life you're living isn't real. Don't get too involved. It's not your home or your family."

"That's a very harsh way of putting it," Judith flushes, "but I get your point."

"Guess who's just phoned!" Miriam calls out from the house.

"Your mother," they answer in unison.

"Indeed. My ban's lifted. She and Uncle Ben are coming to visit next Thursday afternoon."

"Sorry to spring this on you, Judith. You were looking so tranquil."

"Tranquility," Judith says, "is not my natural state, though I do feel more at peace with myself than I've been for years."

She does not add that every time she hears a car in the driveway, or a ring at the door, her heart beats wildly. Visits from Nathalie are fraught with anxiety. They usually go to her bedroom and draw the curtains. She had expected the Special Branch to call soon after her arrival, and when they had not, she assumed they were watching her in other ways. She imagines strange whirrings on the phone, she's certain the house is being watched, and runs to her room whenever an unknown vehicle comes up the drive. Twice she had seen a car turn up the sandy strip, go as far as their driveway, then turn back. An airletter from a friend in England had arrived with its edges unstuck and crudely closed with Scotch tape. She's trying to persuade herself that as long as she does nothing to contravene her banning orders and house arrest restrictions, she has nothing to fear.

"I'll be off," Nathalie says. "Remember what I said, Judith."

"How could I forget such wise, sensitive advice. Bring the next lot of newspapers soon."

5

Every morning rain clouds appear behind the hill, and by noon they've been dispersed by the north wind. Judith sits in the mottled shade of the pergola, her nose and throat aching with dryness. She watches the sap gather like tears on the pruned twigs of the grapevine, grow big, then spill on to the garden bed. A mild breeze moves through the purple bunches of wisteria at the far end of the pergola, releasing waves of perfume that sweep across the veranda, mingling with the smell of sweetpeas and stocks. She draws a deep breath of contentment. It needs only a thunderstorm to clear the air of winter dust.

"Judith!" Miriam calls from the lounge. "Visitors!"

Judith hurries into the lounge and sits as far as possible from Molly's chair. When Molly strides into the lounge, followed by Uncle Ben, panting and pale, Judith stands up awkwardly and walks over to her.

"I'm pleased to meet you," she says, offering her hand.

"I can't return the compliment," Molly replies. Judith flushes and withdraws her hand.

"Ma! How dare you speak like that to my guest, my friend? I don't approve of your silly Zionesses, but I never insult them."

"Unlike you, I say what I think. I've nothing against Miss, uh, personally, but I believe that if one lives in a country, one should abide by its laws. If one doesn't, one gets what one deserves. And innocent people shouldn't be dragged into it."

"Sorry Judith. I didn't realise my mother would make a scene."

Judith sits down, close to tears. When Molly goes out of the room, she feels a light hand on her shoulder.

"You shouldn't be upset by Molly, she's an impossible woman," Ben says quietly. "Such good laws she and her narrow-minded ladies observe. There's fighting in Vietnam, starvation in Biafra, wars all over the world, and what does she say when they don't mention Israel on the radio? 'No news!' Can you take notice from such a woman?" He collapses onto the chair next to her.

"I gather you're not a Zionist."

"God forbid! I'm an atheist. With them it's a religion. I believe there should be only menschen, people, like we say in Yiddish, not nations. And the best way to make good human beings is to do away with nationalism. If there is such a being as God, which I seriously doubt, I would say this to him: next time chose someone else. We've had nothing but trouble since you chose us. And for what? For suffering."

Judith smiles.

"You think I'm mad." His good eye twinkles; the other is hidden behind a frosted lens. "That's the sort of thing I say to irritate my sister. I'm not an ardent Zionist like she is, but I believe Israel must exist, at least while other nations exist."

Molly returns to the lounge and sits on the high-backed chair at the other end of the room. Judith appears to be unaware of her.

"If there was anybody here to receive it," Judith is saying, "I'd turn in my Party card. If I had one. Czechoslovakia, on the map of Europe, looks like a tiny squirrel in the belly of a huge iguana. What harm would her liberalisation have done the Soviet Union?"

"You talk like a child," Ben says patiently. "The Czechs threatened to break up the whole Warsaw Pact. Anarchy they were making, not freedom. It was not the time for freedom of the press, for making protests, for digging up old heroes like Masaryk, may he rest in his grave. What should the Russians have done? Let the Czechs destroy the Revolution?"

"If you have to maintain a political structure with the aid of foreign tanks ..."

"Anarchy is a dangerous sickness. One sneeze, and others catch it. In Poland the students were out in the streets, in the USSR there were underground presses, in East Germany they were jumping over the wall. All organised by capitalist agitators. The ordinary people were happy under Communism."

"I'm surprised at you, Uncle Ben," Judith says. "You sound like a Pravda editorial. I thought you were an independent thinker."

"Tell me your opinion when you are back with your comrades in England. It is very hard to resist the Party Line."

Molly Goldin is looking at Judith with new interest.

"Beware, Judith," Miriam says, "He may be an agent provocateur."

"So, where's it democratic?" Ben says. "In England? They're the biggest hypocrites of the lot. They give arms to the Nigerians and food to the Biafrans, who are killed by British bombs."

Bernard joins them for tea. His novel, he tells his mother-in-law who enquires about it as one would after a terminally ill relative, is coming on well. If he can keep up the pace, it will be published in April. Molly Goldin shrugs; she has scant respect for academics, and even less for writers. But at least he isn't political.

When Judith hears a car coming up the drive, she picks up her crochet bag and hurries out of the room.

"You draw them like a magnet, Ma. We haven't seen them since the last time you were here."

"Do you think they saw Judith in the lounge with us?" Bernard looks uncomfortable.

"No." Miriam watches two strange men approach the front door. "The light reflects off the window. You can't see into the lounge until you're close up. I've tried it."

She glances at her mother who has gone pale and still. Ben sits back in his chair, fingers entwined, waiting for the show to begin.

"I'm Captain de Klerk, and this is Lieutenant Van der Pohl," the stouter of the men says when Miriam opens the door. "This is a routine call, to introduce ourselves to Miss Fletcher. We're from the Regional branch. She falls into our district. Is she home?"

"Of course she's home, she's under house arrest. Shall I call her, or will you speak to her in her room?"

"Privately. This would constitute a gathering. Does Miss Fletcher join you when you have guests?"

"No."

She leads them down the passage and knocks on the door.

"Two gentlemen to see you, Judith. From the Regional Branch."

Judith opens the door. She looks tense as they walk into the room.

Why do they always come in pairs, Miriam wonders

as she walks into the lounge where everyone is sitting in silence. And why does number two never say a word?

"Thank you, Mrs Nathanson," Captain de Klerk says when they reappear ten minutes later. "Sorry for the disturbance. Just a routine visit. Miss Fletcher's in our district, you see, so we had to introduce ourselves."

After they drive off, Judith comes in, smiling nervously.

"You're right, Mrs Goldin. I'm sorry. It's wrong to involve innocent people. I should never have come to stay."

Molly says nothing; she is watching Judith's hands.

"A reflex I developed in jail," Judith says, holding out her trembling hands. "I make a point never to smoke in front of them. I sit on my hands."

"You're too thin, my dear. Miriam doesn't feed you well enough."

"I've never eaten so well in my life," Judith responds.

"If they come again while I'm here," she bursts out, "I'll give them a piece of my mind."

"Don't," Ben advises, "you need every piece you've got."

"And those shaking hands," Molly ignores Ben, "you're no more capable of making a revolution than I am of, of …"

"Of holding your tongue, dear sister. And that's exactly what you should do if they come again. Try to remember you're Chairlady of the Houghton Branch, not the Special Branch. I was in the middle of a story when you interrupted me," he says petulantly. "As I was saying, in Lithuania we all belonged to the Workers' Party. Once a month a comrade would come from Kovno to lecture and to arrange study circles. He kept us supplied with books. I should never have come to South Africa."

"If you hadn't come," Judith says, "you'd have been massacred by the Nazis."

"Leave this country," Ben pats her shoulder awkwardly. "You'll be happier in England. You're not much of a communist anyway. In any other country you'd be a vishy-vashy liberal. And when you're back in London, send my love to Princess Margaret and Twiggy."

After they leave, Judith sets out on her daily walk across the ridge. Aloes snag her skirt and thorn trees scratch her legs as she climbs over the slanted rocks. She watches the rain clouds drift in from the south, casting dark shadows over the veld. Aridity and dust; colour and fragrance. It's easy to be seduced by this oasis in the veld. But the reality is out there. Judith looks west towards the city. Beneath the cranes, between the ridges, the city vibrates with palpable excitement. It is boom time. The stock market is soaring and everyone talks about flotations, going public, new issues, bulls and bears. Even her isolated outpost at the Nathansons had been infected by money fever. We should buy shares, Bernard had said the previous day. The whole English Department is doing it. Ari Feinstein, Henry chimed in, bought de Beers with his barmitzvah money.

Judith listens to the sound of distant thunder and watches the sky flicker with sheet lightning. Does it really matter to law-abiding citizens whose shares are rising daily, that the power of the judiciary is being eroded through laws that bypass the courts; that the completion of a prison sentence for political offences no longer ensures one's freedom? Has anyone noticed that the Terrorism Act was passed the previous year, and that people could be committed to indefinite detention without trial if they were merely suspected of withholding information about acts of terror? Terrorism had been defined as an act committed with intent to endanger law and order in the country. Only the Minister of Justice needs to decide what and who is dangerous. The accused has to prove his or her innocence. If found guilty, the sentence is death. There had been no need to define "terrorist"; if he was on your side he was a freedom fighter; if he was against you, he was a terrorist.

The thunder grows louder, the lightning more fierce. A cool wind drives the clouds towards the hills. Judith stretches out her arms and turns her face skywards. The first drops sting her sun-warmed skin, then the rain pours down, soaking through her dress, running down her body into her shoes. She gasps, delighted, and breathes in the smell of damp earth and wet grass. The clouds pass over, the sun comes out, and steam rises from the rocks and the parched soil. Judith runs down the hill, soaked and exhilarated. This is where she belongs. Her stay with the Nathansons has been a healing interlude, but now she is ready to act, within the country.

Mary, the Nathanson's maid, meets her at the door as she takes off her shoes.

"Miss Judith, you'll catch double ammonia!"

"This is my first true baptism, Mary. I've always believed in the holiness of water."

"Miss Nathalie is waiting for you in the lounge."

"I'll have a quick shower. Please ask her to wait."

Nathalie is pacing up and down the room when Judith comes in.

"You've read all the newspapers, you've caught up with your lost years, and now it's time to leave. Have you booked a passage to England? Have you applied for an exit visa?" She stops and looks keenly at Judith. "My God! You're planning to remain in the country!"

"Sit down, Nathalie. You're making me dizzy. I can't apply for an exit permit until I get an entry permit into Britain. I've been phoning the consulate and they've promised it'd be through any day now. It's difficult to book a berth by phone, so I've applied for permission to go into Johannesburg."

"For a moment I was convinced you were thinking of staying. I'll get you a list of available berths tomorrow."

"Suppose I decide to stay on. I'd find a flat in Hillbrow, get a job at Vanguard Books. Rita Jacobs is under house arrest and she lives alone."

"You're not Rita Jacobs. You'd be off your rocker within days. This has been a peaceful interlude, as you keep saying, and now you're healed. Sort of. You've got to get out of the country or you'll be back in jail before you can say John Vorster Square."

"There's a chance of doing something here. In England I'll become part of the exilic community, and that'll be the end of any real political action."

"Bound and gagged, cabin'd and confined. And at the slightest infraction of your bans, back in jail. Is that what you want, martyrdom? The Nathansons can exist here because they live in isolation, and because they've decided that personal relations are the most important thing. At least Miriam has; Bernard finds an outlet in his writing. So she looks after her children, her servants and stray dogs. She was a fine pianist before she married Bernard. Even if you write, it won't be published here. You've been banned and listed, spray-painted out of existence."

"How do you exist here? I know how you feel behind your tough talk."

"I can live here because I'm a good hater and don't have great expectations from people. I expect the government to be authoritarian bastards, and I expect the whites to cower and conform and keep their heads in the sand. I get a painful sort of pleasure from seeing everyone live up to my twisted expectations. Tomorrow I'll bring you a list of available berths."

"You never speak about yourself, Nathalie, except in slighting or cynical terms."

"What is there to say? Life grows duller and grimmer as you grows older. Especially if you're living without illusions." Nathalie's eyes fill with rare tears.

"What's happening with Helen? She hasn't phoned for weeks. I can understand her not coming here, but she could at least phone."

"She's uh, been busy." Nathalie looks away.

"During her holidays? Nat, you're a poor liar. I understand her well and won't judge her."

"She's got a good chance of getting a passport and wants to avoid complications."

"Oh dear. I complicate everyone's lives. I'm pleased she's getting a passport. Tell her we'll make up for lost time in England. No point in hanging around, as you say. Enquire about bookings, Nat, and I'll write for my exit permit this evening."

"Have you thought about what you'll do in London?"

"Not really. Teach, perhaps. It'll come to me when I'm there."

The phone rings and Miriam runs in from the garden.

"What? Have you phoned the doctor? The ambulance? I'll be right over."

"It's Ben." She picks up her bag and goes towards the door. "His chest seized up and he can't even breathe with oxygen. Aunt Tillie's phoned for an ambulance. He's got to get to hospital immediately."

"I'm coming too," Judith says.

"You can't. My aunt lives in Johannesburg. If they come or see you in the car ... You can't come."

"You're a nut," Nathalie says. "You're looking for trouble."

"See you later."

They arrive before the ambulance. Tillie is standing on the veranda, looking out for the ambulance. She's been crying. Ben is sitting at the window. The loose dry skin of his throat balloons and recedes against his prominent Adam's apple as he gulps down air.

"Sit." He motions Miriam and Judith to chairs. "Pass ... oxygen."

Judith watches him draw air into what is left of his lungs. A small breeze seems to refresh him and he draws a deep breath.

"Better." He knows the breeze only cools his face. After a few minutes, however, he regains colour and his breathing is less jerky.

"This is ... life reduced to ... Remember talk ... about freedom? The Czechs. Who's free? ... I'm not even ... free to die. Too frightened to pull out ... the tube that ties me like a dog ... to oxygen tank. Not even ... free to die ... let alone live."

Judith and Miriam stay with him until the ambulance arrives. They watch the burly ambulance orderlies carry him out on a stretcher. Tillie will travel with him in the ambulance and Molly will meet them at the hospital.

"Regards ... to Princess Margaret and Twiggy ... remember?" he says to Judith as he is lifted into the ambulance. "Leave ... No sense here ... And stop smoking."

Two days later he died. Miriam did not allow Judith to go to the funeral.

"For our sakes. We'd all be aiding and abetting, as they call it. Ben knew you cared for him."

On the afternoon of the funeral, Judith walks aimlessly over the hills. It is a beautiful day. Masses of pale lilac jacaranda flowers emerge from the green anonymity of the suburban trees below her. There will be rain later that afternoon; the clouds are massing in the south. And the steam will rise in the streets, releasing the heat of the dry hot days which preceded it. Somewhere towards the end of this concatenation of ridges is the Westpark Cemetery. Soon they will be lowering Ben's cold, emaciated but no longer suffering body into the warm red earth. She rarely thought of death, and had never before cared greatly where she would be buried. But now she knows that she herself will never lie in this red earth. Ben, too, had had no choice. He would have preferred to be buried in the rich black soil of the old country, the soil that had been soaked with the blood of his people.

There is no freedom, not even in death.

6

"You're going through to Captain Fuchs," the telephonist says.

Judith's fingers tighten around the phone. She has been trying to reach him for over a week. He never returns her calls. Her British entry visa has arrived, a berth has been booked, and she has even received permission to visit her parents in Grahamstown on her way to board the *Dorchester Castle* in Cape Town. All she needs is her exit permit. Although she realises that withholding the permit is the final punitive act, it nevertheless creates the intended anxiety.

"Captain Fuchs speaking."

The curt, familiar voice hits her ear like a physical blow.

"Judith Fletcher here. I'm leaving in two days and have not received my exit visa. I can hardly leave without it."

His soft laugh evokes the gleam of white teeth in a cold, bare room.

"Fletcher, Fletcher. Don't you trust us? You know we wouldn't do anything to delay your departure."

She does not reply. The "Fletcher" is deliberate, provocative. She will not be drawn into an argument.

"I know. When will I receive the exit permit?"

"You're weak on civics, Fletcher. We don't issue exit permits," he says amiably. "That's the job of the Ministry for the Interior. But I'm certain you'll receive the visa before you leave. Thank you for calling. It's nice hearing from you. A sign you bear no grudges. Good luck. And don't befoul your own doorstep again."

She is trembling when she puts down the phone. She had hated him more than any of the others. She even preferred the sanctimonious sadism of Van As.

It is a fine hot day. The Nathansons have gone to swim at a neighbour's house and will not be back for a few hours. This is her last opportunity to walk up the hill. Her suitcase is packed and stands at the foot of her bed. Her overnight bag lies open on the chair. She need add only her pyjamas, toothbrush and towel.

She has said goodbye to Helen and to Nathalie on the phone. Helen's voice had sounded thin as she mumbled apologies for not having visited. Don't apologise, Judith told her. We'll see one another in England. Don't come to the house, she begged Nathalie. It's difficult enough on the phone. Visit me in London. Enjoy your freedom, Nathalie instructed. Without guilt, if possible.

That leaves only the Nathansons, Mary, and Matthew the gardener. Matthew had always been polite, but she knows he does not approve of her. He always looked at the floor when she spoke to him, replying in monosyllables. After three months at the Nathansons, she knew nothing about him except that he was married and his wife was a country woman who lived in the rural areas with their four children, all September babies: he took his leave in January. Mary, on the other hand, a tall dignified woman from Mozambique who is working illegally in South Africa, often spoke to Judith about her children who were being brought up by her mother. Her stoic attitude to hunger, illness, poverty and death was almost too painful to bear. None of my children call me mother, she told Judith. I am osie to them, sister. One day my grandchildren will call me mother.

Judith puts on her walking shoes and sets off along the sand road towards the hill. Her face is damp from exertion when she reaches the top. She sits on the sun-warmed rocks, looking at the veld which stretches away to the mine dumps in the south. It is the veld she will miss most, not the lush gardens of suburbia: the long sweet grass which rings in the change of season. Now the grass is supple, green, filled with sweet sap. Late summer gilds the outer sheaths, and the first frost rusts them. In autumn, the erubescent veld takes fire from the sun. It is then that the cosmos, harbingers of winter, bloom, their white, pink and mauve flowers sparkling like jewels in the red grass, swaying in the chilly April breeze. As the icy winds sweep over the high veld, blanching the rustling grass to pale gold, the veld fires begin, reducing it to dry black stubble, rimed with frost on winter mornings. And with the first rains, the green shoots appear once again, starting a new cycle. She will never again be part of this seasonal rhythm.

She walks to the southern side of the ridge. There it is: the City, cupped between two ridges with its ever-changing skyline and the cranes swinging against a pale blue sky. She turns away abruptly and runs down the hill. If she looks back, she will turn into a pillar of salt.

She does not stop running until she reaches the sand road. Her heart beating painfully, she walks towards the house. In the driveway stands a white Valiant. She hurries into the lounge.

Miriam, looking flustered, sits in an armchair with Zorba and Bouboulina at her feet. Opposite her, on the sofa, sit Van As and a short wiry man with a thin black moustache. They stand up when she comes into the room.

"Sorry, Miriam. I was not expecting guests." She looks at them, nods, and sits down on the edge of Molly's chair, with her hands under her thighs.

"You're looking well, Miss Fletcher," Van As says. "It must be the fresh country air."

"Indeed. The fresh country air. Dark, dank rooms do nothing for one's complexion."

"Actually, we've come to deliver some papers." Van As is visibly disconcerted by her tone. He opens his brief case and produces a large brown envelope. "Your exit visa, and a few instructions about regulations you must follow till you reach the ship. You understand, of course, that you must go direct to the station from here. And when you reach Grahamstown, go straight to your mother's house. And while you're with the family, report daily to the police. You must also inform the officer-in-charge when you leave for Cape Town. And report to the police before you go on board."

He sits back and smiles benignly at Judith.

"Well," he says when she remains silent, "we kept our promise. We didn't bother you at all while you were here, out of deference for Mrs Nathanson. We knew you were in good hands. We must thank you for your cooperation, Mrs Nathanson."

Miriam is astounded by Judith's blatant animosity, and horrified by Van As's suggestion of complicity. Judith meets her startled look with a reassuring grin.

"Well, yes," Van As says, getting up from the sofa. "That's about it. Except to say goodbye, Miss Fletcher. Don't think we don't sympathise with you. We know your family has been living in South Africa for over a hundred years. It must be very sad to be leaving the country forever …"

"Don't count on that, Lieutenant," Judith interrupts in a harsh, clear voice. "It's not forever. I'll be back. And who knows, I may even be issuing you with an exit visa."

He had been on the point of extending his hand to her. He turns away abruptly.

"Thank you again, Mrs Nathanson. It was a pleasure to deal with such a lady."

"I'm glad you called personally," Judith says, remaining on the chair. "I might otherwise have regretted leaving the country, even for a short while."

Van As picks up his briefcase and, doffing his hat as he passes Miriam, walks quickly out of the lounge, followed by Sergeant Smit.

Judith gropes around in her bag for her lighter. "That's the last time they'll darken your doorway, Miriam. Unless you blow up a pylon."

"That's exactly what I'd like to do. Your complexion at the moment isn't as healthy as the Lieutenant would have it. You scared me. I thought they'd haul you off to jail on the spot. Your voice was so firm, so sure."

"There's power in your mother's chair."

"I was nauseatingly polite. Did you hear him thank me for my collaboration or cooperation or whatever he called it? I nearly died of shame."

"They do that. Old tricks. He wanted me to feel unloved, betrayed. Ah well, that was a good way to end off the old year."

"Judith, I feel bad that we're all going out tonight. Pippa is particularly upset. She doesn't want to come with us. But we always see the New Year in with Jeffrey Rider, from the Classics Department."

"It's easier this way. This year, like many before it,

will come in without my help. I'll be fast asleep long before the gong strikes twelve."

Later that evening, Judith watches them walk across the moonlit path to the car. Bernard, tall and stooped, has his arm around Pippa's shoulder, Henry is strumming on his guitar, and an exuberant William is pulling Miriam along. She turns and waves to Judith.

The moon casts a pale green light over the lawn, the trees, and the flower beds, and a heavy scent of honeysuckle and jasmine drifts in through the window. An expectant silence hangs over the suburb. Through the wall of pines, she hears the muffled roar of passing cars. Somewhere a dog is howling at the moon.

Judith draws the curtains and takes a little bottle out of her toilet bag: she will not fall asleep without a little help from her friends. She dabs cream over her face, puts a few pin curls into her hair, and climbs into bed, pulling the blankets over her ears.

When she hears the wailing, she thinks it is part of the violent riot she was dreaming about. She sits up, listening carefully. There it is again: a long full-throated wail, followed by a reverberating, sepulchral sound which she eventually identifies as a telephone pole being struck by a metallic object. Then the air fills with chiming, hooting, ringing and clanking, above which rings the sound of human voices: Happy, happy, happy!

She goes to the window, fully awake. The sounds come from far and near. From the servants' quarters, she hears ululations, accompanied by tins being beaten, whistling and banging. The whole suburb seems awake. The backyard door opens and two figures, dressed in long flowing robes, flit across the lawn.

"Happy, happy, happy New Year!" the cry echoes through the dark scented pines.

Judith clutches the slender bars of the burglar-proofing, and leans her forehead against the impaled iron birds. In the distance the tumult rises and swells like a choir. Voices and sounds interweave, reverberating through the trees echoing through the rocky hills, and piercing the ear with the roar that lies on the other side of silence.

Epilogue

"Fasten your seat-belts ..."

Judith stretches her legs and moves her seat to an upright position. The plane's progress is charted on a computerised image. Against the lilac background is a pale green landmass: Africa. Trailing a red wake, a white plane streaks from Nairobi, to Dar es Salaam, to Harari, to Maputo. Destination: Johannesburg. Ground speed: 880 kilometres per hour. Altitude: 8536 meters above sea level. Temperature: minus 30.

She had requested a window seat. I want to see the African veld, she told the hostess. Your first visit, Ma'am? No, she had replied. My last. The plane breaks through deceptively soft sheepskin clouds, tinged with early morning light, herded by the wind into infinity. Below lies the ecru veld, scarred by red sandy roads, dotted with bush. The sight pierces her heart more truly than the sharpest dagger. She is coming home. Home, home, home, Judith repeats the word like a mantra.

No one will be waiting for her at the airport. Not for her the scenes of jubilation that greeted the return of the first exiles: green, black and gold banners, songs, toyi-toying. She is content to return without ceremony. Home. She circles the word with awe, fear, longing. After twenty-two years in exile she still has to discover where home really is. The change in political fortune had caught her unprepared.

— It is possible to live in exile, she had told Nathalie when they met in London three years after she left South Africa, but not to die in exile.

She had been depressed at the time. Earlier that week she had fallen down a flight of stairs at the school where she was teaching.

— You don't die from a sprained ankle and a dislocated shoulder, Nathalie replied.

— How about a dislocated heart?

— That is another matter.

She wanted to know how Judith managed when she was ill. Who shopped for her, cooked, cleaned? Judith had shrugged.

— I manage.

— Where are all your Comrades when you really need them?

— Spread all over London, surviving, like me.

— To quote an old enemy: many comrades, few friends, Nathalie had said.

Later she had made friends, among colleagues, neighbours, at the local pub. There had been lovers too, but no permanent relationship: a trade unionist, a wild Irishman, a younger man.

She lost contact with the Nathansons after a few years of desultory correspondence. At first, she heard about them through Nathalie. Later, when William came to live in London, she had full coverage on the family. After the success of Bernard's novel, he had left Miriam for one of his students. Miriam blossomed. She went back to university, completed a B.Mus., interrupted by her marriage to Bernard, continued her studies, and was now lecturing at the university. She sold the house of the impaled birds, and was now living with the cellist of the trio she regularly performs with. Lawrence, the son Judith hadn't met, immigrated to Israel where he married a Palestinian woman and served a stint in jail for refusing to do army service on the West Bank. Molly Goldin, the Zioness, must be turning in her grave. Henry took up a scholarship at the Juilliard School of Music, and plays the double bass in the Boston Symphony Orchestra. In his spare time he plays in gigs. Much more fun, he wrote to William. Judith receives a birthday card from Pippa, the mother of three children, every year. After graduating as a speech therapist, she had married and immigrated to Vancouver.

And William, dearest Willie, eventually left South Africa as a war resister. She had seen him often in London, where he is making a name for himself as a cartoonist and an illustrator. He is one of the few people who knows she is Jennifer Crane, writer of children's books; he had been her illustrator. The partnership started twenty-two years previously, when she'd been house-arrested in his parents' home. She told William tales of Africa, and he had illustrated them on any blank surface that presented itself: school books, refrigerators, bathroom tiles.

Between moments of intense loneliness, between teaching and political work, Judith had started to write. During the dark northern winters, she had invoked visions of the veld under cloudless skies; craggy hills covered with aloes, protea and dombeya, the wild pear, and had populated the hills with dassies, honey badgers, tortoises and aardvarks, the lesser animals of the African bush, about whom the San and other native people had woven myths.

Her first story, still unfinished, had been about a solitary bushbuck who is driven into the Kalahari desert by a pack of hyenas, and who wanders aimlessly along the verges of the bush, its heart pierced by the dry grass of the veld. Her books are well reviewed, but she has clung to anonymity. They are cathartic, keep her sane, but she still does not think of herself as a writer. They had also supplemented her meagre teacher's salary and launched Willie's career as a book illustrator.

Most of the Nathansons had flown north; she was flying south. Johannesburg will seem empty without them. But not all the household has flown. Matthew, the gardener, on a pension from Miriam, went home to tend his own garden. And Mary, who had left her own children to be a nanny to others, is looking after her grandchildren in a house Miriam helped her build.

She often wonders what Uncle Ben would have said about the collapse of the Soviet Union. It is not socialism that has failed, he might have said. People have failed. She recalls his quizzical smile when she wept over the Soviet Union's invasion of Czechoslovakia. When you are among your comrades, he had predicted, you will find it difficult to resist the Party line.

She will spend as little time as possible in Johannesburg; there is no one she wants to see. Helen is teaching in California, and Nathalie has moved to Cape Town, where she is the editor of a glossy magazine. Johannesburg is a place of shadows and bad memories, a source of nightmares that followed her into exile. She wonders what role Van As and Captain Fuchs will play in the new South Africa. A sinister one, no doubt. Inquisitors are always in demand, in any system. In this great outburst of repentance and forgiveness, they too may be forgiven by the Truth and Reconciliation Committee. But not by her.

Enough of the past; the future is sufficiently daunting. There is much to be done before a "new" South Africa emerges from the grip of the oppressor. This is the last time I'll use that cliché, she vows. I must loosen up my language, my thinking. Perhaps she had clung to political jargon to distinguish Judith Fletcher from Jennifer Crane. Her children's stories are lucid, fresh, flowing. She has come back to Africa to discover who she really is: Judith Fletcher, political activist, or Jennifer Crane, writer of children's books. It may be difficult to disentangle them, to make a choice. But she will have to play it by ear, the instrument on which she has become a virtuoso.

"Ladies and Gentlemen, we shall shortly be landing at Jan Smuts airport. Please remain in your seats until the plane comes to a stop. We hope you have enjoyed the flight."

Judith looks out of the window. The veld has given way to the crowded, treeless township of Soweto. On the horizon lie the mine dumps. The city emerges behind them in a milky haze. Further north, emerald suburbs tilt towards the plane, and swimming pools sparkle in the sun. At 1,982 metres, the wheels are released with a thud, the plane straightens out over the runway, and lands at 1,524 metres above sea level. The screen blanks out.

Everything has changed. Nothing has changed. She is home again.

*If you would like to know more about Spinifex Press
write for a free catalogue or visit our website*

SPINIFEX PRESS
PO Box 212 North Melbourne
Victoria 3051 Australia
<http://www.spinifexpress.com.au>